To David
on Rwt
Rcc

CW00429849

Reflections On The Sea

Vol 1: Duty and Honour

Ian Tew

Proof Copy
To Be Corrected !

Table of Contents

1.

Civilian in a War Zone

We were sitting in the cockpit, the usual bottles and glasses on the varnished table, after a rather fiery curried beef supper. We needed a drink to quench our thirst. It was a hot evening and the day had been even hotter with little wind. There had been excitement in the bay, smoke pouring from a motor boat. We motored hard, lowering the sails, but arrived after the lifeboat, and our services were not required. We stood by for half an hour, 'just in case, you never know with fires,' said the mariner, but the lifeboat crew were efficient and were soon towing the casualty, the smoke stopped. We were anchored well off the beach, 'don't want our peace disturbed,' said the mariner, but the sea was calm and there was no swell. There had been almost no wind for days.

'Reminds me of the Gulf War, the Iran Iraq conflict the apogee of Richard's salvage years,' said the mariner, refilling his glass. He took a sip. 'Yes fire at sea is the seaman's worst enemy,' he paused and closed his blue eyes, which were emphasised by his very white hair and beard, as though withdrawing into himself. We were all quiet, expectant, knowing a reflection, a memoir of the sea was to be told.

The lawyer, more gaunt than normal, 'it has been a difficult year,' he said in his rather thin voice, was sitting back with his eyes closed holding his glass.

The banker reached forward, his plump face glistening, 'my year was good,' he told us, and poured from the bottle.

The military man, his white hair rather long, no longer serving, was sitting upright with his arms outstretched, his glass on the deck by his right hand. I was the youngest and my glass was full.

'Richard told me about the first of the Gulf war casualties many years later when we met in the Pacific on our yachts a long way away from the Gulf, anchored in some remote atoll miles from anywhere. I was not involved in this particular salvage although of course I knew about it, who didn't in the marine world.

'Richard told me he was at a marine surveyor's party in Singapore, feeling a little down. He had enjoyed a most intense and thrilling six months behind a desk, yes behind a desk can be exciting, but it ended. This is what happened.'

* * *

I was running the company while the Managing Director was on prolonged sick leave, and I say without boasting, very successfully. He called me while I was in Djibouti, after bringing in a third casualty from the Red Sea in as many months and told me to return to Singapore immediately, 'don't argue do as you are told for once,' he said and terminated the call.

I got my own back for what I thought of his bluntness, but he was a man of few words, petty it seems now, by flying first class and spending the night in one of the most expensive hotels in Paris, the Paris Athenee. I walked into his office in Singapore and he said, 'I am dying, they have given me three months, I am flying to the UK tonight and going to a specialist hospital. It's all yours.' He got up and walked out, a man of few words as I said.

I was utterly flabbergasted, no warning, never in my wildest dreams did I think I would be running the company, ships and tugs I knew, but companies? I sat in his chair and thought for a few minutes, what am I going to do? The office was cool in the air conditioning and the curtains were drawn, shutting out the bright sunlight. It was an immense challenge, but how to start. Treat it as a ship, I thought at first then it hit me, pretend you own the company and act accordingly. It all fell into place and an intense, exhilarating six months ensued with an almost vertical learning curve at first.

Well he did not die, he got better, and there he was at the party, glass in hand, fruit juice I discovered because he no longer drank alcohol, large as life. No wonder I felt down, he had taken his old position back and I was to assist him, No2 not No1.

The telephone rang and as I was standing near it I picked it up even though I was in someone else's house.

'I want Captain Richardson,' said the voice which I immediately recognised.

'Speaking,' I replied, surprised.

'Operations said you would be there. Loaded tanker on fire, said to be sinking, south of Kharg Island, hit by an Exocet missile.'

'We don't have anything in the Gulf,' I said. 'The Dutch are there and the Greeks I think, our nearest is in Djibouti.'

'They all declined. The owners offering Lloyds Open Form no cure no pay. The other salvors say she is unsalvable.'

'Well I suppose we could go and have a look, we have an arrangement with a tug company in Bahrein,' I said cautiously.

'Accept the LOF, it could be a first, salving the unsalvable,' the voice laughed. He knew me too well, he was challenging me.

'OK we accept,' I said more loudly than necessary and I put the phone down with a bang.

I looked up from the phone, the room was silent, the guests and surveyor were all looking at me.

'What have you accepted,' asked the newly returned Manager.

'LOF on burning tanker south of Kharg Island, the Iranian loading terminal in the War Zone said to be unsalvable.'

'On your bike,' said the manager and all the marine people, drinks and oysters in their hands laughed. And that is how the most intense few days of my life started, lived not just on the edge but almost hanging off of it, every fibre of my being alive, everything more real, heightened, death might be at any moment from the tanker exploding or another missile. Nothing before or since has surpassed that intense alive feeling, but I am ahead of myself.

We ran a smooth operation and I was on a plane within a few hours arriving the next morning in Bahrein, the smells and colours completely different from green Singapore. Even the arrival had been hazardous, the tension rising each time the pilot tried to land, aborting it three times. It was a crowd of most relieved passengers who entered the arrival hall. Within a few hours I was on a tug en route at full speed for the burning tanker. Pass the bottle.

She was only a small tug, the "Atlas", a midget really compared with my last command, fit only for towing barges. The taciturn captain was not a salvage man, not really interested although I tried to enthuse him with some sort of enthusiasm, one needed positive people on a salvage.

My first sight of the casualty was a plume of smoke rising high into air seen from miles away. There was not much wind and it appeared thicker as we approached rising almost vertically. The nearer we came the odder she looked with the bow well up in the air, the bulbous bow visible which it should not have been since the tanker was loaded. The stern was underwater and quite clearly the engine room was flooded. The fire. Oh! The fire, it was like something out of hell. It burned with a white heat, an intense white heat at its base and engulfed the whole accommodation at the stern of the ship. The flames rose above her, pulsating as though it had a beating heart. I quailed as I took in the sight and thought, not for us and it's the War Zone as well. The tug captain looked mournful and kept shaking his head although he did not say anything. I was on the small bridge with him.

We circled the burning tanker, having to pass well astern to clear the flames burning on the surface of the sea. Obviously she was leaking her cargo of crude oil as well as burning it. I discovered during our long approach that she was not moving suggesting something was holding her in place. What little wind was blowing from the bow to stern keeping the flames back from the main cargo tanks.

I did not have any of my own salvage people with me so was alone, there was no one I could discuss the situation with. The longer I looked, we were hanging off the port side, the more I thought, it might be possible, she is stable, if we can keep her bow into the wind and the flames clear of the cargo tanks… I was well into my forties, the impetuousness and invincibility of youth had gone but I was better able, with my experience, to weigh up the risks. My burgeoning confidence was swept away when I thought if the wind changes the flames will blow forward and she will blow up or another missile might be fired at her. Not for us, a voice kept telling me. We can do it, don't be weak, here is your chance of a lifetime for a world first, to salve the un-salvable, and in a war zone too. My two sides were fighting, the adventurous and the sober sensible. You realise if you take this on the whole company is at risk if it goes wrong. Yes, said the adventurer, but the rewards outweigh the risk. I took a deep breath and said to Atif the captain, we will salve her, call the office on the radio. He shook his head but complied. Pass the bottle.

It was the biggest risk I ever took in my life and the most dangerous. The first six days and nights were without any sleep at all living on the edge, well, almost over the edge. The fire burned and burned fed by the cargo leaking from a tank, broken by the missile explosion, into the flooded engine room. She was hit by two missiles, one in the engine room which caused it to flood and the other in the cargo tank which started the fire. The oil burned on the surface of the water in the engine room, the accommodation making a perfect chimney. All the portholes in the front of the accommodation were blown out and glowed red from the fire inside, the occasional flame flicking out and licking the bare metal, the paint long burned away. It glowed and pulsated like a living thing with a life of its own, terrible in its intensity. Flames would shoot up high above the bridge and funnel into the cloud of smoke which hung over the burning wreck and the noise. The roar of the flames was continuous, rising and falling like gusts in a storm. At night it was spectacular, the whole aft part of the ship glowing in the darkness, and the bright flames above with a stream of flames astern, the sky cloudless with the stars shining brightly. For me it was the most intense experience of my life, every fibre of my being on edge knowing it could all end in an instant. Any sudden noise made me start, although I tried not to show it, and once someone slammed a door and we all fell onto the deck where we were standing thinking another missile had arrived. Once I made the decision I did not falter, my confidence did not fail me whatever the setbacks. It was so important to keep up the spirits of the people knowing the awful danger we were in. At first we fought the fire from the tugs I had assembled. The "Atlas" towed ahead, her taciturn captain grown in stature, willing and cooperative, to make sure the wind was always blowing the flames astern.

The technical details don't matter now, but it required organisation to charter the fleet of tugs and supply boats bringing out foam and personnel, keeping a check on everyone, the constant tension, persuading, cajoling, leading the men until at last my own people arrived from Singapore. My hero, yes, I unashamedly say my hero, Juanito, a brave and resourceful Filipino who accepted the challenge to join me when all the Europeans declined to come. He arrived with his team of picked men and the salvage was transformed, I knew we were going to be successful.

I was the first man to climb on board the burning tanker and tip toed along the deck trying not to make any disturbance. The fire was roaring astern, so fierce the accommodation structure had started to melt and taken a list to starboard, bent like a tree in a gale of wind, the glow inside palpitating like a beating heart, throwing flames out of the empty portholes. I was still walking carefully when I entered the forecastle store. It was cooler in there and I stood for a minute taking stock when I felt a furry thing curl round my bare leg, I was wearing shorts. I went rigid with fear and leapt into the air my mind full of unimaginable horrors, we knew one man was missing and some had died. 'Miaow.' It was the ship's cat. I felt utterly drained and then laughed, waiting for my racing heart to return to normal. Pass the bottle.

I picked him up, yes the cat turned out to be a Tom, and walked normally down the deck knowing how ridiculous my fears were, and handed him over to the crew of the tug alongside.

As time progressed more fire-fighting tugs arrived. My only source of communication was the radio on the "Atlas" to the office in Bahrein who relayed my messages to Singapore and theirs to me. We teamed up with a Dutch company who had a specialised foam fire-fighting tug and she arrived along with her Dutch crew which included a radio room and operator. A Jumbo jet was chartered to fly more foam out from Europe because we purchased all the available supplies in the Gulf.

Six days after my first arrival all was ready for our first and I prayed last foam attack. My salvage crew worked well with the Dutch on board the burning ship with handheld equipment and hoses, a common purpose. They walked into the accommodation when the foam from the tug fire monitor guns had partly extinguished the flames, coordination was the key and the bravery of the men. We were successful and with the flames gone the continuous roar ceased, the silence was strange.

Inside the burnt out accommodation all fittings and paint had burnt, only bare metal was left, and much of that was twisted and buckled into modern art sculptures, quite surreal. The whole edifice leant to starboard some of the metal had part melted in the terrible heat.

You would have thought with the fire out all our problems were over, but not a bit of it. I put one of the chartered tugs to join the "Atlas", she had been continuously towing for six days. We had no big tug on site, so I put five more tugs, two on the port and three on the starboard side, for the tow out of the War Zone to Bahrein. None of us could understand why the casualty moved so slowly despite the combined horse power and we came to the conclusion a piece of the hull had blown out and was hanging off the bottom of the ship dragging along the sea bed.

I enjoyed my first sleep in six days but after a couple of hours was awoken for some emergency and was amazingly instantly awake and able to make decisions. My nerves were bar taught like overstretched strings on a violin, the permanent sense of danger was still with us, we could still be hit by another missile. I only catnapped now until we finally arrived in the anchorage off Bahrein, watched by United States warships.

Our flotilla was joined by our super tug "Vanguard" which steamed at full speed from Djibouti but had been delayed by a crew change. At last I was in direct communication with Singapore and my own salvage people were with me. I immediately transferred my headquarters on board our salvage tug, what a relief. Our divers who were part of the crew of the "Vanguard" were sent down to find out what had impeded the tow. They reported it was not metal hanging down but the stern anchor which the explosions managed to dislodge and cause to fall into the sea. It was trawling along the bottom. We had dragged it all across the Gulf!

At last I was able to sleep and slept the sleep of the exhausted. When I awoke I came off the intense high, the living on another plane where nothing mattered except the fire. Eating and drinking were automatic, almost unnoticed, as was the heat, my entire life's focus was on extinguishing the raging inferno and the tow. Everything seemed less important now, food and drink became more important, doing anything required more effort. I tried to watch myself that I did not allow myself to fall too low. Never again have I ever experienced such an intensity of living, being alive.

The salvage became routine, we were out of the official War Zone, but the tanker war did not stop and more vessels were hit. We chartered two tankers, one small and one large, and ran a shuttle service to unload the casualty. The weather turned against us and there were days of full gale making it uncomfortable on the tugs. I sent the smallest into Bahrein. It was dangerous to relieve the men on board the tanker working the portable pumps discharging the crude oil.

Another ship in ballast was hit further north but out of the official War Zone. The whole Gulf was now becoming the war zone. I abandoned the salvage, leaving it in the hands of my deputy, while I took our super tug and salved the new casualty on fire and abandoned by her crew. We put the fire out and she was towed to Bahrein.

Almost at the end of the discharge a much larger tanker, twice the size in fact, was hit and set on fire also outside the War Zone. Again I raced off with the "Vanguard" and together with the Dutch put out the fire. I towed her to the anchorage off Bahrein to join our other casualties. It was indeed an intense and exciting time of many months, but I did not reach the high I achieved for the first casualty, even when a tanker was hit close by but luckily the missile did not explode.

These salvage operations in the Gulf were the highlight of my salvage years, eclipsing even the typhoon salvage in the South China Sea, indeed they were the highlight of my life. Don't forget I am a civilian, yet here I was in the War Zone for many months, salving ships deliberately damaged by war-like acts. The danger was very real not just perceived. One of our tugs the year before was hit and seven of our people killed. Later in the war another was hit with further loss of life.

I eventually returned to Singapore but life seemed hum drum and drab, the intense excitement, that living on the edge was gone, it was as though my flame of life had somehow become diminished, smaller, burned less brightly, nothing seemed really important again.

* * *

The mariner was quiet and we were all silent. I never heard him speak like that before, it was so vivid I felt it was almost as if it was him who was the salvor as though he was reliving those events which occurred over twenty five years ago. It was as though the first war casualty and subsequent months had been too intense for normal life to be lived happily as though something more was needed to sustain the soul.

Nobody said anything, absorbed in what had been said.

The yacht lay quietly at her anchor in the calm, the beach now almost invisible as we went below for the night, the anchor light bright in the darkness.

2.

The Telephone Call

The wind blew down the gully in sudden gusts, causing cats' paws of white on the dark river water and the evergreen trees to rustle and flutter. The yacht heeled to port and starboard depending on the direction, swinging at her single anchor.

'Reminds me of Steepvalley,' said the usually uncommunicative lawyer, his thin face vague in the oil lamp light, his grey hair almost invisible.

We were down below to escape the rain, noisy on the cabin roof. It was dark, early for summer, and the low cloud and encompassing dark green trees emphasised the blackness. The banker, the mariner, the navy man, and myself settled back on the cushions waiting in anticipation for the lawyer to continue. The varnished table dully reflected the oil lamp flame illuminating the nearly full bottles.

'Yes, Steepvalley in winter, I went there.' The lawyer continued in his rather toneless voice. 'I have forgotten why I picked the place, I suppose because it sounded a bit different. The pub was on the harbour front, the White Lion or some such name, and had views over the harbour. I was in need of a short break having won an important case and I was exhausted. I booked myself in for a weekend.

'I caught the train to Bideford, which involved a change somewhere. I forget now, it's a long time ago all this happened, but I remember because I hate having to change, be it trains or planes. A taxi took me to Steepvalley down the back road, which is very narrow and steep. It ends at the seafront outside the harbour and in front of the hotel, the headlights of the car illuminating the dark pebbled beach. The taxi driver told me the village high street was barred to traffic. The whole village and harbour was owned by one family and had been for a couple of centuries.

'I got out of the taxi on the lee side. It was pitch black and blowing a gale, the rain sweeping in from the west. I entered the hotel through a most unprepossessing entrance, the doormat wet, and went into the large reception hall with a small lounge leading off it.

'I was not best pleased to be shown to a small anteroom up some vertical stone steps apart from the main building, and demanded a room in the hotel itself. It all turned out satisfactory in the end. I enjoyed an excellent dinner sitting by the window in the restaurant overlooking the harbour, not that I could see much in the darkness and driving rain, just the faint outline of some small fishing boats. There was the occasional thump as a large wave hit the breakwater.

'The next day at breakfast I sat at the same table with a better view of the harbour. It was as light as it was going to become in winter and I looked around.

The gale had blown itself out and it was quite a nice wintry day, but cloudy. I did not see the sun, and I wondered if it actually rose above the precipitous cliffs behind at this time of year. The harbour was much smaller than I had imagined, a mini harbour really, a small cove protected from the sea by the breakwater with the white painted hotel at the land end of it.

'I climbed up onto the harbour breakwater using the steps outside the hotel. There was still quite a swell running in, and the pebbles on the beach rustled as the waves swirled in the corner between it and the breakwater. Out to sea and to the west a ship was anchored, and I thought it was an odd place to be, although she was probably sheltered from the westerly winds. There was no shelter from the north-west. She was quite a large cargo ship about 7,000 tons gross her derricks neatly stowed and the accommodation amidships.

'I left the breakwater and climbed up the difficult and uneven cobbled steps to the street, the stones were the colour of the pebbles from the beach. It was quite dim, the village enclosed on either side by the gully or small valley in which it was built.

Once was enough, and I spent the rest of my time in the hotel. The small lounge was very comfortable and it had a few books in a good-looking book case. It started to blow again in the afternoon not that I really noticed it.

'That evening, I was sitting in the snug bar, enjoying a pre-dinner sherry when someone rushed in from the cobbled yard entrance and shouted, 'There is a ship in trouble,' and at that moment, the lifeboat maroon went up. Nothing to do with me, I thought, but the lure of the sea, the need to know, overtook me and I went outside into the cobbled courtyard and walked down to the front of the hotel. Of course I could not see anything; the ship was outside the harbour hidden by the tall breakwater. It was sleeting and cold, but even in the darkness I could hear the seas sweeping along the outside of the harbour wall, sometimes coming over the top, sending the spray high into the air, the light from a non-curtained window, lighting the water droplets. I could hear the occasional noise of a pebble falling, picked up by a wave and flung over the wall, very different from the thump of the wave hitting it.

'The lifeboat was being towed by a tractor into the sea, the ramp remarkably sheltered. I saw it speed off its cradle and was lost to view as it rounded the harbour entrance.

'I went back into the hotel through the bottom bar, and up to my room. The window faced the harbour, and although one storey high I could not see further than the harbour wall. I went down through reception where a couple of people were in animated conversation and out through the main entrance. I walked the few yards to the breakwater, climbed the steps and stood on the wall with my back to the hotel.

'It was raining heavily with occasional sleet and blowing very hard indeed. The hotel wall just gave me enough shelter so that I could see the ship had dragged her anchor. I did not know if they had the second anchor down but she was far too close to the harbour wall, her lights glowing hazily. The lifeboat was close to her on the shore side but not alongside. I noticed from my earlier observation that the tide was flooding, the wind and tide were in tandem. The waves were sweeping down the side of the ship and it was impossible for the lifeboat to go alongside. The ship was pitching heavily and snubbing at her cable which I imagined was bar taut.

'Suddenly there was a great white light and I saw the lifeboat had switched on her searchlight. It would ruin their night vision. I could see both anchors of the ship were down, and the chains were both bar taut. If one chain broke she was finished. The darkness was even more intense when the searchlight went out. I watched carefully and saw she was slowly dragging. It was very slow, but it was quite apparent that the bearing was changing from my stationary position. She would just clear the harbour breakwater and fetch up on the beach to the east. If something was not done quickly, she was doomed.

'I stood in the cold miserable conditions wet through, my London raincoat not much good, buffeted by the storm. The light had illuminated the sea. It was a seething mass of white, the tops of the waves blown off. I was mesmerised watching what seemed to me, the inevitable loss of the ship, and perhaps those on board her. It was like Schadenfreude, that German word, gaining pleasure from watching someone in trouble and I felt somehow ashamed but I did not move.

'Without warning the navigation lights of quite a large ship, or so it seemed in the difficult visibility, appeared, approaching from the north west. I could see the red sidelight of the lifeboat, and its white mast light with the anchor light of the doomed ship ahead. I saw the green sidelight of the approaching ship and her two white steaming lights. She seemed to be heading for the stern of the anchored ship, moving quite fast. Suddenly she turned. The two steaming lights closed, came in line and the red sidelight appeared. The steaming lights opened again, and the green sidelight went out.

'I could only admire the magnificent seamanship of whoever was handling what I presumed must be a very large tug. She swept past the doomed ship very close and continued until quite a long way ahead. She stopped, and only the stern light was faintly visible, masked by the wet weather, but it was difficult to see exactly. The spray from the tops of the waves was mingling with the rain and sleet.

'She was moving backwards, her stern closing the bow of the doomed ship. There were shapes on her low after deck, and I could see men on the forecastle of the casualty.

'Suddenly there was a bright flash from the stern of the tug and a rocket flew onto the forecastle of the casualty. I could not see the line, but I imagined it must have landed from the movement of the men. The lifeboat moved ahead, and then shone its searchlight on the gap between the tug and the ship. I wondered if the tug captain was annoyed his night vision was affected, but perhaps he was far enough away for it not to matter.

'I could now see a rope being heaved onto the casualty followed much more slowly by a wire. The taut anchor cables were clear of the tug, which presumably is why the searchlight had been switched on. If the propeller hit a cable it would be the end for the tug as well.

'In what seemed a very short time, the tug had connected and moved ahead and angled slightly out to sea, while I could hear over the storm the clank of the chain cable being heaved up by the casualty one after the other. The tug was taking the weight of the ship. The anchors were soon aweigh. The tug and casualty moved slowly ahead and were very soon out of sight to sea, swallowed up by the rain and spray-filled darkness.

'I went back into the hotel through the snug bar, the few drinkers abuzz with the saving of the ship. I finished the sherry I had left on a table and went up to my room feeling very cold. It felt very odd as I changed into dry clothes almost as though the drama I had witnessed in the storm outside was a figment of my imagination. It was a perception, not real.

'I enjoyed an excellent dinner and slept well that night. I had a quiet Sunday returning to London on the Monday.

'On Tuesday I returned to the office refreshed and somehow invigorated from the weekend. I was given a new instruction, a salvage case. I was very surprised, yes, even shocked to discover it concerned the drama I had witnessed over the weekend. I was to act for the tug owner. The solicitors who normally represented those salvors were the long-time solicitors for the shipowner. They could not act for both, in those days there were no Chinese walls. So we got the case, and it started my association with that salvage company because they instructed us in some future cases.

'It was some months before I had the opportunity to interview the captain of the tug, which started my association with Richard. The tug was in Falmouth, and it was at the end of that cold spell, the ground covered in snow, giving the West Country a completely different look.

'The Lloyd's agent who met me at the station took me to the town public marina, where there was a rubber boat with two Filipinos. Their faces were covered with balaclavas, and they were dressed against the cold. It was a fine winter's day and I felt rather incongruous in my London suit and blue overcoat as I was helped into the boat by the smiling Filipinos and sat on the rubber side. The driver, a young man, smooth faced with long hair falling down to his shoulders was wearing a balaclava scarf and some kind of coat. The driver grinned, as his crewman took my briefcase. He spoke into the radio around his neck as he backed out of the berth, turned and headed out into the harbour increasing to full throttle. The boat seemed to jump out of the water and I had to hold on for dear life, all dignity gone, my briefcase sliding aft until it was stopped by the fuel tank. The bowman was standing up holding onto the painter as though riding a horse. Luckily the water was smooth, but she almost took off over the wash from a returning fishing boat. The young driver's hair was flying behind his head and he shouted at me,

'"You like?" and laughed.

'The tug from the marina had looked large, but as we approached her at speed, she appeared huge in my sight and I thought we were going to hit her. At the last moment the Filipino turned the boat, flinging water onto the tow deck, and stopped her, the engine screaming as he put it full astern. There was no gangway at the tug, and I had to scramble over the gunwale, helped by a burly Filipino, who I later discovered was the bosun.

'I knew that when she was built, she was the largest tug in the world. My admiration for the man who had manoeuvred this huge ship off Steepvalley increased immensely.

'Richard was on the tow deck, as I stood collecting myself and the driver of the rubber boat handed me my briefcase grinning.

'"Enjoy the ride out," said Richard in his soft but clear voice.

'I did not know whether to be angry or laugh at my being humbled and said, "Bit different from the agents launch," and then seeing the still grinning Filipino driver laughed and said "exhilarating."

'"Rene is the best small boat handler I have ever come across and he has nerves of

steel," said a smiling Richard as he led me into the accommodation.

'His cabin was nothing less than stately and covered the entire width of the accommodation, bathroom, bedroom, dayroom. It was luxury indeed. I was served not a mug of tea, but from teapot with milk in a jug and cup on a tray. I was surprised at the standard of service for a tug.

'Richard was still under fourty, smooth shaven, his face still comparatively unlined, his most distinguishing feature was white hair, which made him look older, very useful sometimes, but I am getting ahead of myself.

'This is Richard's account from which I made his statement, recording all he said on my dictaphone, taking notes on my legal pad and times from the logbook.'

* * *

We were anchored in Milford Haven. I made a run from Falmouth, out into the Irish Sea, but the casualty did not require assistance, so I decided to shelter from the forecast gale. I was able to go anywhere I liked in the United Kingdom without telling anyone except obtain permission from the harbour authorities and that was purely a traffic control matter. What I could not do was to leave UK waters without clearing out from immigration and Customs. I was a foreign flagged vessel, and I found it very interesting that I was able to proceed around the coast as I wanted, a complete godsend for a salvage tug.

We were in the cove at the western end of the harbour and could use the zed boat to run ashore to the pub. It was late afternoon and dark when Ricky my radio officer called me and said there was a radio telephone call. I went up onto the bridge, and waited our turn for the call.

'Is that the captain of the tug Gibraltar?'

'Yes,' I answered intrigued by the female voice.

'Gold Ranger is in trouble anchored off Steepvalley and needs urgent help,' said the tense but controlled voice slightly overly loud.

'What is wrong?' I asked briskly, my pulse racing.

'She has disconnected,' said the male operator.

What an odd thing, I thought as I walked over to the chart table. Yes, there was a Steepvalley, just across the Bristol Channel, about 45 miles away.

It was blowing hard from the southwest and it would be a rough crossing, but I was in command one of the biggest tugs in the world so it was no problem. But could I leave on such flimsy information; perhaps it was an elaborate hoax. I thought of radio telephoning the salvage brokers, but knew they would be on to me as soon as they had any information, they would want to earn their commission. I thought of telexing Singapore, but knowing the old man and manager they would say it was up to me, and if they had any information they would have telexed me already. The only negative I

31

argued to myself was the cost of fuel, and I dismissed this out of hand. We were a salvage tug.

'Tell the Chief Officer to stand by forward,' I instructed my new young handsome third officer, who was doing his best to impress me in what for him was a completely new environment, he'd been in tankers. He was improving, and might be quite useful in the future.

I rang down to the engine room and told the engineer on watch we would be leaving shortly. The engines were on short notice and being continually warmed through. Shortly afterwards, I heard the deep throated cough, as one after the other the two powerful diesel engines were started.

Roger the chief officer was forward heaving up the anchor and after obtaining permission to leave from harbour control I steamed out of the sheltered port, past the Heads and out into the Bristol Channel, increasing speed all the time. It was very dark with low cloud and the visibility was reduced by the rain and sleet. As soon as we cleared the shelter it was rough, very rough. The Atlantic rollers topped by breaking waves rolled into the Bristol Channel and the 'Gibraltar' rolled and pitched heavily, the seas and swell on her starboard quarter. It was a slow roll that never seemed to stop. At first I thought something was wrong, she went over so far. At the end of the roll she hesitated, as though reluctant to come back and then slowly righted herself. It took a little getting used to, and this mingled with her pitching made for a most unpleasant passage. I eased back and eventually decoupled one engine. Proceeding at full speed on only one engine, made her much easier but most of the crew were seasick. I can't say I blame them. I considered I had a cast-iron stomach, but felt queasy. During the crossing the wind had veered and there was a touch of north in the westerly.

It was very dark when I approached the casualty, the low cloud, rain and sleet and close proximity of the high cliffs making it more so. I observed from the radar that she was close to the harbour breakwater. I would have to pass to the seaward, there was not enough room inshore, she was so close. I had made my plans with Roger, and the crew were all ready as I headed for a point astern of the anchored but slowly dragging ship. It was blowing very hard indeed and as we closed the land the sea and swell went down a little but the altered direction of the wind meant there was almost no shelter. I would have to be quick if I was to save the Gold Ranger. I needed speed to manoeuvre the big tug in the prevailing conditions. When I was close on her starboard quarter I turned at full helm, the Gibraltar heeling with the tightness of the turn shipping water on the after deck. I headed into the wind and parallel to the heading of the pitching casualty. I slowed down as the tug swept past, her crew lining the starboard bow, while my people tried to throw lead filled heaving lines to them but despite the weights the wind tossed the lines away. I continued forward of the Gold Ranger guessing where her anchor cables were leading and when well clear ahead told Roger on the walkie-talkie to let go of the starboard anchor. It was blowing, far too hard for him to hear me shout, and with the low cloud scudding eastwards it was dark as sin.

Once the tug was brought up I used the engine and bow thruster to keep her heading into the wind, Roger went quickly aft leaving the second officer to stand by the anchor.

Roger had already prepared the Schermuly rocket equipment in the shelter of the winch room. I had switched to the aft control position and stood with my back to the rain and sleet too busy to be cold. I could see the entire tow deck and watched Roger move out on the inshore side, the port side, take aim and fire. His aim was good. It went straight downwind, the line landing on the starboard bow of the casualty, where the willing crew picked it up and heaved over the messenger line then more slowly, the heavy wire forerunner. The lifeboat standing by shone her search light and I could see we were well clear of the taut anchor cables, she had both anchors down. It affected my night vision, and I told the third officer on my radio to instruct the lifeboat to turn off the searchlight. The connection was quickly made.

The Gold Ranger started to heave up both anchors. I kept weight on the short tow wire and the casualty moved forward, making the chains slack so it was easy to heave in. It took all my concentration to keep the tug ahead of the casualty and in position, instructing the second officer when to heave in the tug's anchor.

The last bit was very difficult, keeping the tug and Gold Ranger in position while she heaved home each anchor, in turn. As soon as the second anchor was off the sea bed I headed out to sea.

I returned to the bridge shaking, but whether it was from the relief of tension or the cold I was not sure. Mickey the mess man was waiting for me with dry clothes and a mug of tea. I wanted sea room and deep water when the bosun slacked out the tow wire to its almost 2,000 feet length.

'Why you not wear the oilskin I leave for you,' grumbled Mickey, his shape just discernible in the dark wheelhouse.

'Thanks Mickey,' I laughed taking the towel he handed me. I quickly changed into dry clothes, watching the sea and swell through the revolving clear view screen.

When the bosun had secured almost the entire 2000 feet length, I slowly increased speed, feeling much better, heading into the sea and swell. Mickey picked up my wet clothes and left the bridge.

Once clear of the land, it was very rough, but at slow speed the tug, helped by the stabilising effect of the taut tow wire was quite comfortable. The Gold Ranger followed well, until we turned south in the morning, when she yawed to one side and rolled nearly as much as the Gibraltar.

The tow proceeded well, the weather moderating later in the day. I took her into Falmouth and with the aid of the harbour tugs put her alongside the Falmouth dockyard. Once the tow was disconnected and the gear recovered I put the Gibraltar alongside the jetty ahead of the Gold Ranger. It was dark when I went on board.

The very grateful overweight Greek master signed my Lloyd's open form and termination letter at the same time. He offered me a drink, which turned out to be a very fiery spirit with my coffee.

'Tell me Captain,' I asked, smiling when the formalities were over, 'why did you do not send out a distress message?'

'Owners,' he mumbled shaking his head his jowls wobbling his hands waving from side to side as though trying to chase away some imaginary image.

'I had a telephone call over the radio but the lady did not say who she was, just the Gold Ranger is in trouble.'

He looked distressed and said looking me in the eye, 'no matter for you your Lloyds form signed you okay.'

I saw a very worried and unhappy man.

'You must not say about the telephone call,' he urged.

'But that's ridiculous. I must say how I heard about the casualty about your problem.'

He remained silent looking down at his feet his shoulders slumped and would not say anything further, and that was that.

* * *

The lawyer ended picking up his nearly empty glass.

'Very interesting,' said the mariner, 'that is what Richard told me when I met him in the Pacific, however he told me a little more. Richard did not leave the Captain's cabin straight away, and this is what he told me.'

* * *

'Tell me Captain who was the lady and why did she radio telephone my tug?'

I pressed the slumped man.

The captain looked up, his cheeks wet with tears, and I saw he had been weeping.

'Okay, I tell you if you promise, no swear you are keeping secret.'

I remained silent.

'I trust you,' he cried and stood up and I thought he was going to weep once more, but he pulled himself together and said again.

'I trust you. My owners very difficult people. I tell them have engine problem and need tug. They say, tell engineers to fix, that is what they paid for. Engineers say cannot fix need spare part. I tell owner, and they say, you anchored you ok. We will send spare part may be two or three days. I say very bad weather ship in danger need tug. They say no tug. What can I do? If send distress, I lose my job. If no send distress ship end up on rocks. I lose my ship and maybe my life and crew lives. But owner, he don't care, he got insurance. What to do. I ring my wife on radiotelephone and order her find tug. Send to me, but not say who she is. So owner never know. Okay, you no tell.' He looked so forlorn and dejected.

'Ok Captain I will not tell anyone.' I held his shoulder and shook his clammy hand.

I pondered on the vagaries of human behaviour, when the cabin suddenly seemed to be invaded with the agent, owner's rep and dockyard personnel.

I stood back and the captain put on a good face welcoming everyone offering refreshments. I slid unobtrusively out of the cabin. I had my Lloyds form and termination.

I never let on what the captain told me and maintained I did not know who had called and given me the information. The captain in his evidence maintained he did not know.

'The Gibraltar was like a gift from God.'

* * *

The mariner ended. It was late and the bottles were empty. It was blowing a full gale and the yacht occasionally snubbed at her anchor heeling in the gusts.

'Well well,' said the lawyer, 'so that is how it happened. Richard never told me, he just said he received a telephone call and acted on it. The outcome was very satisfactory for us. It was a very good award. The owners appealed of course. We counter appealed saying it was not enough for the dangers involved. The appeal arbitrator increased the award much to the annoyance of the owners. This was maybe a year or more later, and Richard had performed more salvage by this time.'

'So he kept faith with the captain. He did not let on,' said the navy man.

'Well, it was no skin off his nose,' said the mariner. 'Pathetic really for a master to be so afraid of his owners still no worse than some politicians and war.'

'He should have told me,' sniffed the lawyer. The banker merely snorted.

3.

The Captain

I took a deep breath and knocked on the door, but there was no answer. I needed the captain on the bridge. The typhoon was upon us and I was very concerned. I knocked again and entered.

'Captain, you should be on the bridge.'

There was a particularly strong gust and the ship heeled, the wind even inside the accommodation howling, which emphasised my appeal. There was still no answer from the recumbent form lying on the settee, dressed in his rumpled shore going clothes. He was curled up in the foetal position.

I shook his shoulder and said loudly, 'are you ill Sir?'

'Go away,' he screamed, the sound shocking in the confined space, the wind shaking the accommodation.

My heart sank and that first flicker of fear, that first feeling of panic started. I was young to be chief officer and this was my first ship in that rank, but I knew I must fight the rising panic inside me. The realisation the captain was in a funk, or mad, or sick hit me and I had to do something about it or we would lose the ship. She was jerking on the too short, a chain cable to the buoy, and the ship would break free. What should I do? I thought hard as I looked at the captain and realised I had no option. I had to take over command, usurp the captain. It was a terrifying concept but once I accepted the situation there was no more time to ponder.

I quickly returned to the bridge. It was raining heavily, the water drops hitting the wheelhouse windows like bullets fired from a gun.

'I'm taking over command John, the captain is in a funk or ill and will not come to the bridge. Log it, I will sign and you witness it.'

The second officer looked shocked. Another strong gust heeled the ship alarmingly, and the bow swung off, brought up suddenly by the chain accentuating the typhoon raging outside.

'We are going to fill the deep tanks with sea water John. Fill in the water ballast order book and the third mate can take it down. I will phone the Chief Engineer.'

While telephoning, I looked out of the wheelhouse window crisscrossed by strips of plaster in case it shattered. The squall had passed and I could see up the harbour. The air was filled with spume and it was blowing so hard the tops of the waves were blown away, making the sea appear white. I could not see the chain but I knew it was bar taught. It was time to use the engine, and I pushed the telegraph lever to slow ahead.

'Steer north,' I ordered the quartermaster as I watched the engine revolution counter flicker then move to 20.

Another gust hit the ship heeling her sufficiently to make me hold on and I knew if I did not do something else quickly the chain would break.

'John, do you think you could go forward and let go the starboard anchor? Take the bosun.'

'I can but try,' his slight frame belying an inner strength and determination. At that moment the chief engineer appeared in the wheelhouse agitatedly waving the ballast book in his hand, his normal unflappable manner gone.

'What's this Mr. Mate?' he said pointing at the instructions I had written. 'It's not signed by the captain.'

'Captain is sick chief, I've taken over command. He is lying on his daybed. I have logged it.'

I felt rather than saw, as I looked out of the wheelhouse window, the "Redshank" was moving ahead. The whole accommodation was shaking in a gust and the air was filled with spume and spray blown off the sea. The noise of the wind meant we had to raise our voices to be heard. I did not want to overrun the buoy and so stopped the engine for a short while and then resumed slow ahead. The chief engineer, ballast book in his hand, stood watching and I said,

'The sooner we ballast her down the better, chief, the eye of the typhoon will pass over Hong Kong and the wind may be even stronger afterwards.'

The door of the chartroom was flung open and the captain appeared, still in his shore going clothes. He staggered in and clutching the chart table for support shouted,

'Everything alright Mr. Mate?'

'Yes,' I replied, shocked.

'Then I will leave you to it,' and he left the chartroom slamming the door behind him.

My steward entered with a tray of tea and sandwiches wearing a life jacket over his uniform. He put the tray down on the chart table and left without a word. The chief engineer followed him out.

Suddenly over the noise of the raging typhoon I heard the rattle of chain, very faint, but I gave a sigh of relief. With the anchor down there was every chance the ship would stay attached to the buoy. The violent swings caused by the gusts would be much reduced, and when ballasted she would be much heavier in the water.

John returned soaking wet but smiling, 'we had to crawl, and were lucky to make it.'

'Well done, well done,' I said shaking his hand, 'you've given us a good chance of making it now. The eye will soon be here.'

The eye of the storm passed over, an eerie calm with a cloudless star speckled sky. I could see the ships in the harbour all appearing to be normal, but I knew we did not have long. I used the engine to try and swing the ship to head in the opposite direction so she would be bow onto the renewed typhoon once the eye passed. Quite suddenly the first gusts of wind and then the typhoon was upon us again with a vengeance from the opposite direction. The bow swung violently, heeling the ship, but the cable held. The wind moaned around the wheelhouse, shaking it, vibrating the windows, causing the whole ship to shudder as though it was trying to detach the wheelhouse and fling it away. The tumult had increased and it was difficult to even think, but I kept the engine on slow and sometimes half ahead guessing when she started to move ahead. The anchor made all the difference and eventually it was over, the wind decreased and life returned to normal. I went down to the captain's cabin, knocked and walked in. The captain I had usurped was lying on his back, and there was blood all over the place, he had cut his wrists. I turned to find the chief engineer standing in the doorway.

'Well Richard, he was a weakling. Now you really are Captain.'

4.

The Lawyer's Case

It was a wild night at the anchorage but it was safe. We were sitting in the cabin, the rigging noisy in the wind, the yacht occasionally snubbing on her anchor. It was early in the year and cold, so the paraffin heater was on, and it was warm below. The single oil lamp gave a soft but dim light in the saloon, the faces around the table in shadow. The half-empty bottle stood on the varnished table, the fiddles up.

'I once had a very odd case,' said the solicitor. 'The skipper of a salvage tug used to drink too much and eventually died of it, but in his heyday, he was a formidable man. He was a good leader and a natural born ship handler and could almost make his tug dance, that was in the days before dynamic positioning. He wasn't tall but he was big, not exactly fat, but you knew he was there. He had a good head of white hair and his exploits were well known in the salvage industry. This is what he told me, and my own involvement will be apparent.'

* * *

I had salved a grain ship off Massawa, a long and difficult job, and towed her to the anchorage. Despite the

45

country's starving inhabitants, the port officials would not let me bring her in, a vivid and personal observation of man's inhumanity to man. It was a long story, but I eventually escaped and went up to Jeddah for bunkers. On the way back to Djibouti we encountered rough weather, yes; it can be rough in the Red Sea. I was going too fast and shipped a sea, short and steep, green over the bow and covering the wheelhouse, the windows completely obscured by water.

'Silly fool, going too fast,' muttered the naval man.

I immediately slowed down. The chief engineer, his boiler-suit half open, his smooth chest bare, rushed onto the bridge, shouting at me, demanding to know what I thought I was doing. Water had gushed down the funnel. I apologised and said it would not happen again. The chief engineer, a thin, taciturn man with thinning hair and a long, cadaverous face, appeared mollified by my apology.

'Well, I'll hold you to that. Don't do it again.' His face, usually unsmiling, broke into a slight grin as he left.

I went out onto the bridge wing, in the bright hot sunshine, where the breaking seas were white and sparkling. I had altered course to have a look at High Island, the western entrance to Abu Ali channel, almost a rock, about two hundred feet high, devoid of vegetation. I was quite close when I noticed what appeared to be a ship apparently close to the shore, to the west of north point on Jabal Zuqar, the big island to the south. The wind was southerly so we were now in sheltered waters and in the calmer sea saw the ship, clearly not a wreck, quite near the shore.

It was an odd place to be, I thought, and slowed right down. I altered course so that I went straight for her, in order to have a better view, leaving High Island to port. North Point was quite clear, low and sandy, and I could see a couple of greenish bushes. The island, which rose to a considerable height, was barren, brown and harsh.

It is almost impossible to describe the excitement and thrill of finding one's own salvage, should she be aground, before anyone else. It does not happen often, maybe once or twice in a lifetime.

The third officer, Pepe, a bright young Filipino, very keen, had taken a bearing and distance off the radar and plotted it on the chart.

'She is aground Captain,' he shouted from the chartroom inside the wheelhouse, his excitement palpable.

Well, I thought, this is interesting. I am going to investigate.

The ship was not showing any distress signals, not even the two blackballs, "ship aground signal", which was odd, to say the least.

I stopped the tug off the small cargo ship, about 5000 tons displacement. The accommodation area, painted white, was aft and there were two large hatches forward. A mast amidships enabled the hatches to be served by four single Thompson derricks, one at each end. The black funnel had two thin white bands, and the hull was painted a light green.

'I'm going to go over and see what's what,' I told Edgar, my chief officer, who had
appeared on the bridge when he heard the engine slowing down.

'Tell the bosun to launch the zed boat. You stay and look after the tug while I go and investigate.'

'Okay, Cap,' he replied, his smooth, moon face, with its sliver of a black moustache, smiling, relishing the chance to manoeuvre the tug when I was away.

I picked up my emergency bag, which contained, amongst other things, the Lloyds
Open Form, the salvage agreement. I unhooked a walkie-talkie from its hook in the chart room, switched on the company internal private radio and walked into the Radio
Room behind the chartroom.

'Keep your ears open, Ricky. There is a ship aground and I'm going to have a look. You've heard nothing?' I asked the radio officer.

'I would have told you, Captain,' he said, looking a little put out, his usual grin missing. Long hours in the radio room, listening and lack of exercise had made him a little plump for his age.

'Of course,' I placated him. 'We won't tell the office anything yet.'

'Okay, Cap.'

I went down onto the tow deck aft and climbed into the launched rubber boat, the zed boat, with Rennie, my skilled helmsman, sitting by the running engine. He was thin and tall but seemed to wrap himself into a small space quite easily. He was very much in command, the small boat his own domain. His long black hair, which he wore loose, gave him a rather Bohemian look, out of place in the present situation. The two divers, both fit and strong, were already in the boat with their equipment. The bosun was an unusually big, burly fellow for a Filipino, and sported a crew cut. He was sitting forward with the second officer, Arturo, who by contrast was thin and slight.

Rennie was obviously relishing his role as we sped over the choppy but sheltered water to the grounded ship, shipping occasional spray. We passed close astern and read her name, *Vilya*, painted in white. No national ensign or other flags were flying. Rennie motored slowly round the ship, while the divers sounded with a hand lead line and marked their findings on a sketch. The water was crystal clear and the reef seemed very near the surface where the ship was aground. There was no sign of life.

We motored back to the aft accommodation and shouted up at the bridge. No one appeared until one of the divers started hitting the hull with the lead and a head materialised over the bridge wing.

'What do you want?' a voice shouted.

'Can I come aboard? I am from the tug and we can help you.'

The head disappeared. Sometime later a rope ladder was dropped over the side from the main deck and the head reappeared.

'Okay, you can come aboard.'

'You come with me, bosun, I may need your strong support, and you get ready to

dive,' I said to the divers.

Rennie manoeuvred the boat alongside the ladder, and I climbed up with the walkie-talkie around my neck and the bag on my back. Once on board I was shown up to the bridge by a surly looking Ethiopian, the bosun following.

'On board,' I said into my walkie-talkie to inform Edgar, whom I had left in charge of the tug.

On the bridge I was met by a big, fat man, who looked very unhappy. Not surprising, I thought, with his ship aground.

'I can help you to re-float,' I told him.

'My engine no good,' he said, not meeting my eye.

There were two Ethiopians on the bridge, one of whom had thrown over the ladder, both apparently watching the Captain and looking very surly indeed. The whole setup looked strange to me, no other officers or people on the bridge apart from the Captain and the Ethiopians. The Captain was a different nationality to the others, I guessed he was Middle Eastern. It turned out he was Turkish. The ship was strangely dead, no noise or vibration, and I realised the generators were not running.

'Okay, you help me re-float then tow.' He paused. 'I tell you where later.' My spirits leaped. Could I pull this one off, find a casualty, sign a Lloyds Form, before anyone else knew about it and then be successful? I could feel my heartbeat increasing, and I had to control myself from leaping up and down.

'First you must sign this,' I said, producing my Lloyds Form from the bag on my back.

'What is this?' he demanded, looking at it. 'I have heard of Lloyds.'

'It is the salvage agreement,' I informed him, hoping that it was not going to scare him off.

'Salvage, eh?' he said. 'Okay I sign, you look like nice man.'

I had to control myself to stop my hand shaking with excitement and joy. It was like winning an ocean race. I filled in the form on the chart table, and he signed it after me. I walked to the bridge wing and hailed the zed boat.

'Make your diving survey,' I ordered.

'Okay, Cap,' replied Arturo, waving his hand.

'Lloyds form signed, Edgar,' I said into my radio. 'Prepare for towing. Making diving survey. Log it.'

I took stock of my salvage. Looking forward from the bridge I could see the two holds served by the Thompson derricks. The steel hatches would be very difficult to open without power, should it be necessary. In her day she had been a modern ship but was now past her prime. The captain was still in the wheelhouse with the two surly Ethiopians.

'What is your cargo, Captain?' I enquired.

'General,' he avoided looking at my eye, 'about four thousand tonnes.'

'Have you got a cargo plan?'

'No plan,' he mumbled. Very strange, I thought.

'The manifests,' I demanded.

'No manifests,' he answered, looking down at the deck, shaking his head, his chubby cheeks wobbling. Even stranger, I thought.

'How about a cold drink while we wait for the divers' report?' I suggested.

'Okay, I get from my cabin,' he said and walked out of the wheelhouse, followed by the two Ethiopians.

'Bosun, something strange about this lot, have a look around and check aft, where we make the connection. See if there are any other crew members about.'

The captain came into the wheelhouse, followed closely by the two Ethiopians, and thrust a glass of tepid water into my hands.

'Something wrong, Captain?' I queried.

'No, no, everything okay,' he responded, avoiding my eyes. The two Ethiopians were listening to his every word.

'You say engine no good, what about generators?' I asked. The ship was very silent, felt very dead, as though the life had left her.

'No, nothing work,' he said, looking quite distressed. He shook his head, his fat cheeks trembling, the whole bulk of him drooping.

I went out onto the bridge wing. The ship was in a small bay, close to high cliffs ahead, bare, brown and barren. I looked at my salvage tug, so smart with her white hull and buff accommodation, low and sleek, very much an ocean-going vessel. Edgar was keeping her close by the stern of the casualty, which was in deep water. I could see the crew working on the aft deck, preparing the towing gear.

The bosun walked along the boat deck; big and powerful, a man to have around in a tight spot, his steps firm and unhurried, confident in himself and his abilities. He climbed the ladder onto the bridge wing.

'I only saw two other crew members who looked like Ethiopians,' he reported. 'The bollards aft are okay, no problem, we should back them up together using some wire I found.'

'No power,' I informed him. 'We will use a messenger through a snatch block and
back onto the tug using her power.'

They would not let me into the forecastle or number one hold. Number two hold seemed to be full of cartons and cases.

'Okay, the quicker we get this thing off the better,' I urged.

At that moment, the divers, drops of water from their wetsuits occasionally hitting the deck, came onto the bridge wing and showed me the sketch they had made. There was no apparent damage, though of course they could not see the bottom where the ship was aground.

'She looks okay,' said Elmo, the senior diver, 'straight pull astern, see?' he pointed
at the sketch. 'Plenty of water aft and up to the grounding area.'

'Well done,' I congratulated them. 'You can take me back to the tug in a minute.'

I walked back into the wheelhouse to find the captain looking at the chart on the chart table. I showed him the divers' sketch.

'No problem,' I said, cheerfully, 'we'll connect up and pull you off. Your crew
can help with the connection.'

'Crew no can help,' he objected.

'Oh, have you sounded the tanks and holds?' I asked.

'No.'

Very strange, I thought.

'Elmo!' I called out, glancing up to where he was standing, looking over the bridge front. 'Find a sounding rod and line and sound round,' I ordered. 'Get the second officer Arturo out of the zed boat to help.'

'Okay, Cap,' he called back.

The two Ethiopians were still close by the captain.

'I'm going back to my tug now,' I told him, 'and I'll send some of my crew over to make the connection. Then I'll leave a couple of my men with you.'

I could see his guards listening intently, and it was with a most dejected look, that he said, 'No.'

I now knew something was very wrong. No captain I had ever come across had behaved like this. The sooner I connected up and had control, the better. I went out onto the bridge wing, and looked down into the zed boat. The bosun and Rennie were sitting there, patiently awaiting my instructions.

Shortly afterwards, Elmo and Arturo approached me.

'We sounded the tanks and holds forward of the accommodation,' they said.

'The holds are dry, forepeak is empty, there is some fuel in number two, and number one double bottom tank seems empty,' said Arturo as he showed me their findings.

'Okay, let's get back to the tug,' I said, climbing down the outside companionway
ladders to the main deck.

Once back on board the tug, I called everyone together on in the tow deck.

'We will connect as soon as possible. Something is very wrong on board, the captain
seems to have two Ethiopian guards, and there does not appear to be a crew.'

'There were four black men in the crew's mess room,' interposed the bosun.

'Okay, bosun, thanks, the captain does not want any of us on board when we re-float, nor for the tow. The divers and Rennie will stand by in the zed boat when we make the attempt and let me know when she moves. The chief officer will take over a party to make the connection. Don't walk around the ship, and stick together. When we have connected, you are all to come back.'

I climbed back onto the empty bridge, followed by Pepe. The engine was running but the propellers were in neutral pitch. I was sweating in the heat of the afternoon, the sun blazing out of pale blue sky which looked like hot steel. The sea to seaward, out of the shelter of the land, was rough with white horses glistening in the sunlight.

The zed boat was soon away with the equipment and men, while the bosun, along with Arturo and the rest of the crew, prepared the towing gear on the tow deck.

It was not long before Edgar called on the walkie-talkie.

'Okay, Cap, we are ready.'

I had switched to the aft control position and walked out into the bright sunshine, leaving Pepe on the bridge. She was a lovely tug to manoeuvre, just the twin screws, no bow thruster, but she had her whims and was sometimes a little unpredictable and wayward. I had to concentrate and feel what she was doing, I could not tell you why I

did anything until after I had done it. She was big and I could not afford to make mistakes. The wind was blowing off the land, however, so off the casualty. It was simply a matter of backing up the stern into the wind, close to the aft end of the casualty.

The best line thrower on the *Vilya* threw the heaving line onto the stern of the tug. The bosun quickly grabbed it, securing it to the messenger and the casualty party heaved it on board, ran the messenger through a snatch block, previously secured, and threw the heaving line back on board the tug.

I kept the stern close to the *Vilya*. The messenger was heaved back and onto the tug winch. It was now possible to heave the heavy wire onto the casualty, where Edgar and his men made it fast into the slip hook, which had been secured to the bitts.

The main difficulty was to keep the wire clear of the revolving propellers. As soon as Edgar signalled that the forerunner was secured, I steamed slowly ahead, while the bosun paid out the main tow wire from the big towing winch. Arturo made sure it was clear, his slim body slightly incongruous amongst the heavy gear. I told the bosun to

secure when we were about a thousand feet from the casualty.

I switched the controls back to the bridge and went back inside the wheelhouse. Edgar and his men were soon back on board the tug. Rennie and the divers returned and were standing by at the forepart of the casualty in the zed boat. Edgar came up onto the bridge. 'We've backed up the bits round the other bits and around the stern accommodation,' he laughed. 'Tow away, Cap.'

I slowly increased power. I had told the captain to listen in to the walkie-talkie I had given him, but I was treating her as a dead ship, as though no one was onboard. The tow wire was beginning to come out of the water as I slowly increased to full power.

'Full ahead,' I said into the walkie-talkie.

'No movement, Cap,' reported Elmo.

Very slowly, I altered course to starboard and the tug started to move sideways through the water, the tow wire bar taught. I slowed down, and the wire slid back into the water.

'Slack another five hundred feet, bosun,' I commanded into the walkie-talkie.

'Okay, Cap.'

Once the tow wire was re-secured, I increased back to full power. The wire now had a nice catenary, a good curve, and the middle was in the water.

I lowered the dolly pins, which held the wire in the centre of the towing gunwale as the wire started to move along the greased gunwale. I turned to port and the tug heeled and started to move sideways through the water, adding the tug's weight to the engine power. I continued to do this, going out on each side of the casualty.

After some time of this, there was still no movement and only an hour of daylight remained. I did not want to re-float at night, as the darkness would add considerably to the danger of an accident. We were on our own here, in the middle of the Red Sea, and would not be able to obtain any assistance if anything went wrong. We were reliant on our own resources.

I started to be more positive and aggressive with the tug, going further out on each
side, closer to the reef, the tug heeling further, a bit of black smoke coming out of the funnel as the engines laboured and I adjusted the propeller pitch.

'Captain, movement,' shouted an excited Elmo over the radio.

I flung the tug back to port to give that extra pull, the tow wire singing, well clear of the water; if I got it wrong it would break, which would be a catastrophe. It would fly back and cause damage to the tug, with a real risk to life.

'Yes, she is coming off,' the radio squawked.

It is now obvious from the tug. I could see the movement so I slowed down, watching the tow like a hawk. I did not want to tow her into the rough water when she was afloat because I wanted the divers down to inspect the bottom. I turned the tug slowly towards the shore as the bosun heaved in the tow wire on the main winch. I then steamed slowly in towards the reef, and the chief officer let go of the anchor. The wind was blowing off shore so the casualty stayed nicely astern of the tug.

Just as the sun was setting, Elmo's voice came over the radio.

'She's okay, Cap.'

'Well done, come back on board,' I instructed.

'Okay, Edgar, get the Yokohama fenders out on the port side and we'll heave her alongside. Send a party over to the casualty in the zed boat with the divers to take and
make fast the lines. Make sure they stay in pairs. I don't trust the Ethiopians.'

Earlier, I had made a report, enquiring after the previous name of the *Vilya,* which we had deciphered on the stern as being the *Rame*. Ricky, the radio officer, brought me a message in response, which read, '*Rame* hijacked Red Sea on voyage to Aden carrying arms and general cargo. Tow to Djibouti.'

My heart sank. Why is it that anything I tried to do was difficult and complicated? So, the captain was being controlled by the Ethiopians. I was surprised they had not armed. Or maybe they did not want to frighten us off until re-floated.

The manoeuvre was completed successfully, as darkness fell, highlighting the barren cliffs ahead, deepening the darkness, making the bay quite eerie and forbidding in the silence. I would be glad to be out and away.

The stern of the tug was now alongside the bow of the casualty, in the '69' position, the aft end of the *Vilya* sticking out ahead of the bow of the tug. The anchor was holding both vessels easily, although I would have to watch it if she swung with a change in the wind.

The bosun was setting up a rope from the bow of the ship to heave up the tow wire, which had been slipped from the *Vilya* and could now be connected to the bow of the casualty. There were four Ethiopians on deck, watching by number one hatch, and the captain still had his minders on the bridge.

When all was ready, I climbed aboard the casualty, taking the bosun with me, and went onto the bridge. The captain was sitting in his chair in complete darkness; my torch was the only light. I could not see the Ethiopians, but I was sure they were there, blending into the darkness.

'No generator, no light,' said the captain.

'Where you want to go?' I asked. 'Massawa,' replied the voice from the darkness.

'Okay,' I replied. 'Here is one of our walkie-talkies with spare batteries, you can call us at any time.'

I handed it to the captain, who looked very dejected, his fat face illuminated by my torch, his minders still shrouded by the darkness.

As soon as we were back on board I got underway. It was not difficult, the lines to the *Vilya* were let go and the anchor weighed. The *Vilya*, or *Rame*, drifted astern while the tug moved ahead. The bosun slacked out on the tow wire, with Arturo watching. Once clear and with the main wire secured, I slowly manoeuvred my tug onto the course I wanted and the tow turned and followed.

I set course for Djibouti when we cleared the islands and increased to full speed, then settled down to wait.

It was a beautiful, starlit night, the heat of the day had gone, the wind had died down, and there was a half-moon. I could see the tow, no lights, in the moonlight, which was following, pitching gently in the residual swell.

Unless he was stupid, the captain would know we were heading South, not North, even without looking at his darkened compass. Would the Ethiopians realize? Were they seafarers? I hoped not.

Before starting the tow, I had been into the radio room to see Ricky.

'It's stay on, stop on tonight,' I said cheerfully. 'I'll give you the position every hour, as requested by the office.'

'Okay, Cap,' he grinned. 'What's new!'

With a salvage in tow, everyone was in a good mood, anticipating a good bonus. Little did they know, apart from Ricky, of the other complications. The night wore on
and I dozed occasionally in the captain's chair. The Ethiopians had not realised, I thought.

'Captain.'

A voice from my walkie-talkie awoke me from my reverie.

'You not heading South.'

'How are you?' I asked, prevaricating.

'The Ethiopians, not happy. They don't think you heading where they want to go.'

'Well…'

At that moment Edgar rushed in from the bridge wing. It was his watch, the 0400 to 0800.

'Pirates! Quick Captain, look!' he shouted.

I rushed out behind him and there in the bright moonlight were two, high-speed military craft approaching the casualty from either side. In the distance, astern, was the outline of a warship.

'Not pirates, Edgar, the Navy,' I laughed, the tension easing. 'We are safe now, or at least our salvage bonus will be.'

I watched through the binoculars as the two craft went alongside, and I could see some men climbing on board. A short time later, a much more cheerful voice said,

'Captain, French people take my ship, thank you, thank you. Bad men locked up, one dead. Thank you!' he cried. His relief palpable, even over the radio.

The warship followed us all the way to Djibouti where we anchored the casualty in the outer anchorage, having sent Arturo across with some men. After slipping the tow, I went alongside.

The captain hugged and kissed me, much to the amusement of the French lieutenant.

'Thank you, thank you, thank you!' he cried.

* * *

'Of course, the salvage company used me as their solicitor,' continued the lawyer, 'and very good business it was, too. As soon as Cassidy, the general manager, received the skipper's first message, I was called and that is when I discovered the *Rame* had been hijacked or, in marine legal terms, pirated. At the arbitration, I was able to show how they had rescued the ship from pirates, and so received an enhanced award, one of the few times it has happened.

'And the crew?' asked the naval man.

'Well, you remember the Ethiopians? Or as it turned out, the Eritreans who would not let the bosun search number one hold? That is where the crew of the *Rame* had been incarcerated with no food or water after she had run aground. They were in a pretty poor state when the French released them, but soon recovered. In Djibouti, it turned out there was nothing wrong with the engines and generators. The Chief Engineer had immobilised them after the grounding, which was deliberate, before being incarcerated. The captain, who was a lot smarter than his appearance suggested, sailed to Aden under his own steam, with his recovered crew, after his owners and cargo had put up salvage security.'

'I'm surprised some enterprising person has never had a go at cutting out one of the Somali pirated ships,' remarked the naval man.

'I'm sure the lawyers would find that it was illegal or breaching the pirates' human rights or some such nonsense,' scoffed the Mariner, stroking his goatee beard.

'And why do you think the pirates captured the ship and wanted her to go to Massawa?' asked the banker.

'I forgot to tell you, the Ethiopians were not real pirates as such, some would say they were freedom fighters. They were Eritreans. They wanted the arms in their fight against Ethiopia for Eritrean independence.'

'And the tug skipper?' asked the mariner.

'Well, this was one of his most unusual salvages when he was at the height of his

powers. The salvage as such was not particularly difficult for someone like that, it was the finding and the pirate element that made it so interesting and lucrative. I met him, of course, in Djibouti, to take his evidence. He was knocking it back after his success but it was almost as though he was in conflict with himself. He lasted, I don't know, another five or six years? The decline was quite quick when it started. Pity. Well, tragedy, really.'

The cabin was warm and snug when the naval man opened the cabin doors and looked out.

'A beautiful night, not unlike the one when the *Rame,* or *Vilya,* was captured by the French. But colder,' he said.

The yacht was now lying quietly to her single anchor.

5.

Voices

'Bad show,' said the major firmly, 'yachts should not be run down.' We were sitting in the cockpit at single anchor waiting for the tide to turn. It was misty and the visibility was less than two miles, the sky obscured, and lunch was on the table.

'It is always a failure on someone's part, often both parties are at fault,' surmised the lawyer.

'The people on the yacht which was rundown in the Channel could not have been keeping a lookout astern,' observed the mariner, 'it was bad weather and understandable but it killed them.'

'The ship should have seen them on the radar or sighted the stern light,' stated the major firmly, his white hair damp from the mist.

'Not easy to see, the light would have been low down near the water and her radar echo may have been hidden in the clutter caused by the rough sea,' suggested the mariner, stroking his goatee beard. 'Reminds me of something Richard told me of an incident in the Red Sea.'

He paused, taking a sip of water.

'It was quite early on in his career and his first sojourn in that area, based in Djibouti, with the old "Malacca", his first command. Various tows and salvage work had bought the tug to the Red Sea, including a visit to Mogadishu. But that is a different story.'

'Hope this fog clears before we leave,' said the navy man, as a bank rolled in obscuring the shingle only fifty yards away, the fog swirling and weaving, the water droplets cold to the skin.

The Mariner continued. 'It was winter, but still very different from this,' he laughed. 'It was warm and pleasant during the day, quite cool at night. Richard was towing some loaded ship he had salved to Suez. He had placed a couple of men on board as running crew to pump occasionally, using the portable generator and pumps they had placed on board during the salvage. There was a small leak the divers had not been able to find in the time available before starting the tow. It was evening, but the sun had not yet set, although low in the horizon. Richard was sitting on the bridge wing, enjoying the evolving sunset, which was turning out to be a good one, sipping from a wine glass which he placed back in the holder welded to the bridge bulwark.

'"Had these welded, soon after joining," he had told me, "need to have a secure place for my glass."

'They had just passed Daedalus Reef, the lighthouse is visible for miles when the visibility is good and this is what he told me.'

* * *

I was enjoying a glass of wine before dinner, watching the sun low on the horizon, and the beginnings of a sunset, when there was a call on the company radio. I placed my glass in its holder and walked the few paces into the wheelhouse, Edgar, the chief officer was answering.

'We heard a voice,' said the sailor on the casualty quite agitated.

'Voice?' queried Edgar rather dismissively, his moon face frowning.

'Yes, voices in the water.'

'Are you sure?' asked Edgar.

'Yes,' said Romeo firmly.

'Ask if they are running the generator,' I said.

Edgar spoke in Tagaloc and shook his head at the answer, his face still frowning.

'It is possible Edgar, Romeo is a reliable man, and it is very quiet on the tow as you know.' I thought a bit and then made up my mind.

'Okay, tell them to throw something floatable in the direction he heard the voice.'

I pulled the electric telegraph lever to half ahead and started turning the tug to star board. I intended to make a wide turn and try to arrive back at the flotsam now thrown over the side, and then slow steam on the reciprocal course. I had thought of slipping the tow, but remembered it had been rigged for a distance tow. She was on chain bridles. I would have to do the best I could with the tow in place. It was deep water, so I was not worried about the wire hitting the bottom. The tow would follow the tug.

The sun was still just above the horizon, a molten ball of lead, so it was still daylight. When I passed the floating life buoy, and some wooden planks on the reciprocal course, Rennie and the divers were ahead in the rubber boat. I had organised lookouts as high up the mast as our most agile sailor could go. And all the crew, including the cook were standing at vantage points, some with binoculars.

There was a shout, almost a scream, from the lookout up the mast, his hand pointing at about two o'clock, on the starboard side.

I slowed to dead slow and spoke in my radio to Rennie in the rubber speed boat while still watching the tow like a hawk. I did not want her overrunning us.

'Go where the mast head lookout is pointing.'

The zed boat veered over to starboard. I could see now what the lookout saw, possibly a head, which I confirmed by looking through the powerful bridge wing binoculars and then I saw a second head.

'Definitely two, maybe a third.' I said into my radio.

Rennie soon found them and willing hands helped them on board the "Malacca" when he bought the zed boat alongside.

The entire crew disappeared, and I decided to wait for the two survivors to be bought to the bridge. Sometime later, wearing bright clothes donated by my generous people they were helped into the chartroom. Two European men, one with a dark beard, and the other quite fair, with a seriously sunburnt face. The darker one had not fared so badly.

The dark one spoke from the settee where they were sitting.

'We were run down,' he said in good English, 'in broad daylight, we were in the water for six hours,' his voice level and emotionless, as though he was telling us he had been out for a walk in the park.'

'Start from the beginning,' I said kindly, pencil in hand. I had to make report, inform the office.

'We were on a yacht sailing from Suez to Djibouti, and we were run down by a very big ship. We were busy eating in the cockpit and simply did not see it.

Luckily we were not down below but the others were not so lucky,' he said in his quiet voice.

'No one keeping a proper lookout?' I asked.

'I suppose not,' he replied, we certainly weren't looking astern, although we were ahead.' The fair one nodded.

'What's your name?' I asked the sunburnt one, his face covered in cream.

'Michael,' he said, his English clear.

'And your companion?' I prompted.

'Jack,' the dark one said and I noticed Michael look surprised. Jack gave Michael a hard look. I wondered if all was as it appeared to be.

Evidently Jack and Michael were travelling together, young men in their twenties, and had persuaded a southbound yacht to take them to Djibouti. Their passports had been lost with the sinking. Jack said they had signed on as crew and had been cleared out of Egypt as normal, when the yacht had sailed and obtained her clearance.

'Then it will not be too much problem at Suez,' I said, 'I know the Harbourmaster and he can arrange things with the immigration who will have the yacht crew list. Your passport details will be on it and you can talk with your embassy and obtain a replacement.'

Neither of them looked as pleased as I thought they would, but I let it pass.

'What were the names of the other people on the yacht?' I asked.

Jack told me and I noted them down on my report.

'How did you manage to survive so long in the water with no lifejackets?' I asked.

'Michael and I are good swimmers, young and fit. I know you won't believe this but dolphins supported us,' said Jack and Michael nodded.

'Amazing,' I said skeptically.

'They came to us about two hours before you arrived, and at first swam around us. We were terrified and splashed with our legs and arms. A dolphin nudged up to me and squeaked as though it was trying to tell me something. I stopped splashing, calmed down and then it appeared the dolphins wanted me to hold on and eventually I climbed on to its back.' Jack told me quietly with awe.

'The same for me,' confirmed Michael, 'I think they saved our lives, they gave us hope. They were heading for that lighthouse you passed. They swam off when your rubber boat came towards us,' he said, tears running down his sunburnt face making little channels in the cream.

'Quite amazing,' I said. I believed them. 'You must be tired, thank you for your details, and see you in the morning. We won't be in Suez until the day after tomorrow, so have a good sleep.'

They left the bridge assisted by some of the crew. It was now quite dark accentuated by the lack of the moon which had not yet risen. The stars were bright in a cloudless sky but we would never have found them in this darkness. I pondered on the vagaries of life, how random things are, how lucky they were to have been heard.

I wrote up my report and gave a précis to Ricky for sending to the office in Singapore. I gave him two more messages, one for our private agent at Suez, and one for the Harbourmaster.

I mulled over what I had heard, the dolphin assistance at first seem seemed some sort of fantasy, but they were very convincing, and I had heard of a similar occurrence.

The voyage towards Suez continued uneventfully through the Straits of Gubal in darkness, passing the barren brown almost menacing mountains, visible at dawn, which seemed to have outlived their souls. Although the tow followed well, I stayed on the bridge. The Gulf is very busy, quite narrow, and full of oil rigs and platforms and collisions are not unknown. It was a head wind and the tug pitched gently. The two survivors stayed off the bridge and out of sight, became out of mind.

We arrived at Newport rock early in the morning. It was cold. I'd been surprised that no message had been received, either from Singapore or Egypt concerning our yacht survivors whom I had not seen since their rescue.

I was much too busy entering port after more than twenty four hours on the bridge to worry about it. I was tired and had to use extra effort and concentration.

Our private Egyptian agents had been very efficient in convincing the state agents to arrange berthing on arrival. The pilot boarded at Newport rock, and we were early enough to go straight to the wharf before the northbound convoy started entering the Suez Canal.

I had to be on my toes, the tow wire had been shortened before Newport rock and was shorter than I liked but necessary for the intricate manoeuvring ahead in shallow water. I would have liked to have changed the connection on the casualty to a simple slip hook, but there had not been time. I sent Edgar and his men across in the zed boat, well wrapped up against the cold, and they had unlashed the chain bridles so they could be slipped quickly.

I discussed with the pilot how we were going to berth, and knowing Egyptian tug masters, persuaded him to agree to use the two harbour tugs just to push the 'Amity' alongside. She was not very big, only about 5,000 tons deadweight and her draught was only 7 meters aft so there was plenty of water in the narrow channel leading to the harbour. There was not much wind this early in the morning and I was quite confident of being able to position the ship off the berth without assistance. I had done it before in Cape Town with a loaded ship I had salved in the Southern Ocean.

During this busy time I had of course forgotten about our yachts survivors. I successfully positioned the 'Amity,' the two Egyptian tugs pushed her alongside the wharf, and she was made fast. The chain bridles were let go and it took a little time to wash and heave them on board. Once this was done, I went alongside the casualty to supply power and other services. It was intended to discharge all the cargo, and tow her to the dry dock for inspection and either repair the bottom or be declared a total loss.

Immigration came on board with the agents. I still had no message concerning Jack and Michael and was now quite concerned.

Our private agent took me to one side and said, 'don't mention the two people you picked up. I have been with the Harbourmaster, and there is no record of a yacht of that name having been in Suez.'

'Jesus, we have illegals.' I gasped.

He laughed and said, 'don't worry, I fix.' Hassan was indeed a great fixer, and it normally took cash preferably dollars.

'Don't say anything about them and don't put their names on the crew list,' he continued.

'They are on the list already,' I pointed out, now seriously alarmed.

'No, you must fill in the official form, which immigration have brought on board.'

And so it was, the tug was cleared in and officially Mike and Jack did not exist. Just as the immigration officials were leaving with their little gifts from the bonded store Ricky handed me a message from Singapore.

'No trace of your yacht, or people. Do not declare them.'

My heart sank, what was I to do now? People smuggling is a serious offence in any country, let alone Egypt.

'What are we to do?' I asked Hassan, showing him the message.

'Keep them on board, until we can fix.'

Well, to cut a long story short the two survivors disappeared, which in a way was a blessing in disguise. There were no thanks for saving their lives and all the trouble we had been through.

It turned out that the yacht had been stolen from the marina in Eilat, at the top of the Gulf of Aqaba, that's the one opposite to the Gulf of Suez. The story, Jack and Michael had told us was a pack of lies, and there were no other people involved. Their disappearance solved a lot of problems. However, I thought they should have thanked the sharp-eared sailor who had heard their shout in the water and thus saved their lives.

Life was hectic, and they faded from memory. It was, I don't know, a year or two later when I received an unsigned letter, undated, no address and typed, which read:

'Dear captain.
Jack and I would like to thank you and especially the man who heard us in the water for saving our lives. We were lucky in Egypt, and escaped, leaving your tug as soon as you went alongside the ship. I would just like to say I was on Her Majesty's Service, and Jack was the same for another nation.'

And that was that, nothing official, the mariner concluded.

* * *

'Well, they were lucky in more ways than one,' commented the lawyer, 'theft, illegal entry, and presumably exit from Egypt. I wonder what they were up to.'

'The main thing coming out of all this is for mariners to keep an all around visual lookout at all times. I must admit Richard sounds a good ship and tug handler,' remarked the navy man.

'He was,' said the mariner. 'The dolphin help was interesting, very unusual, but I have heard of an incident like it before. Presumably the dolphins were trying to reach Daedalus reef.'

'All very interesting,' said the banker.

'The murky world of spies and intelligence,' said the mariner. 'I have managed to keep well clear. I remember Shanghai, in my youth,' and his voice petered out.

'Time we moved,' pointed out the navy man, 'the tide is on the turn and the fog has lifted. We are going to have a good passage after all.'

6.

Death Cry

The yacht was anchored in the sheltered anchorage off the beach and we were sitting in the cockpit, shielded from the bright sunshine by the awning. It had been an enjoyable short sharp sail against the wind with two reefs in the mainsail and a partly rolled up headsail. The remains from tea were spread out on the varnished table.

'Have you ever heard, well I should say experienced the sound, of a death cry?' asked the mariner after a particularly loud shriek from the beach, stroking his white goatee beard, the face ruddy above.

'Death cry, did you say?' asked the major, surprised, rubbing his hand through his full head of uncombed white hair.

'Yes, death cry,' said the mariner, his voice slightly raised and his blue eyes sparkling.

'What do you mean?' asked the lawyer, his long thin face looking perplexed.

'I mean the cry someone makes when they know, not think, but know they are dying or about to die suddenly.'

'I have heard men screaming in agony and die,' said the major, grimacing his face.

'Horrible.'

'No, that's not what I mean. Well – perhaps I will tell you the story,' said the mariner, putting down his mug of tea.

* * *

We were in the Persian Gulf off Dubai making ready a crude oil storage tanker for towage to Singapore, one of those ones where the engine room and accommodation have been cut off, leaving a straight wall-like stern. She was to go into dry dock. I was acting for someone, I can't remember now who, probably for the insurance. I had to inspect the tug and tow and it was the first time I met Richard. The tug, I think it was the "Messina", lay alongside the tanker, only the crow's nest and the tops of the mast were visible, the hull was hidden below deck level.

The Filipino crew were working on the deck of the tanker loading portable pumps and equipment ready for the tow, when I heard this terrible cry, it turned my blood cold. I froze in horror. It was a sound I never wish to hear again. It was a cry, a scream from the soul, an inhuman sound, from someone in extremis, not pain, but experiencing some awful, terrible, unseen horror. They knew they were dying. It is a sound which has haunted me all my life.

I rushed over to where the men were working to find what I thought was a corpse lying face up on the deck inside the safety rails. The sun was high in an unclouded sky and it was hot. His crew mates were looking at him, their faces bathed in sweat, and some were hauling up a stretcher. They strapped him in and lowered the stretcher to the deck of the tug. He looked dead; I could see no sign of life.

Work continued, and it was the next day before I boarded the tug for my inspection. Richard was very efficient, and all was in order. I asked about the dead man, because I had not seen any activity to take the body ashore.

'He is still out, unconscious,' said Richard brusquely.

'You mean he is not dead,' I said surprised, 'that terrible haunting cry.' He did not comment and I left it at that and continued with the job at hand.

It was many years later, after Richard retired and I knew him well that I asked about the man on the storage tanker. We were anchored close by his yacht off an atoll, I forget where, somewhere in the Pacific and I had joined him for an evening drink to enjoy the sunset. He was alone.

'What happened to that man who fell on the storage tanker in the Persian Gulf and screamed that awful death cry? It has haunted me at various times throughout my life,' I asked.

'It was a very odd thing,' said Richard, who paused with his eyes closed, as though looking back in time.

'I was in my cabin, making sure the paperwork was ready for you, when I heard that terrible, awful scream, that death cry. I have never heard it before or since nor do I want to, but I knew exactly what it was, not pain, but the scream of the ineffable, unimaginable, terror of a person who knows he's going to die before he has time to make peace with himself. It was as though the soul was lamenting the coming death because it is so sudden and unexpected. I rushed out on deck expecting to find a corpse. There was nothing until I looked up and saw a crowd of my crew by the rails of the storage tanker looking down, their faces reflecting distress. The sun was bright and it was hot.'

'What happened?' I shouted.

'He's fallen, I think he's dead,' the chief officer yelled back, looking down at me, his face revealing his dismay.

The mess man pushed past me with a stretcher, all deference gone, and I followed, helping him make fast the line lowered by a diver. The stretcher was hoisted onto the deck of the tanker and a diver and sailor climbed down the pilot ladder onto the tug.

Shortly afterwards, with great care, the body was lowered in the stretcher onto the deck of the tug, and the diver and sailor with the mess man protecting his head carried him below. I followed a little later and found the dead man, the second diver, lying in his bunk – but he was not dead. He was breathing so shallowly that one had to get very close to see, otherwise there was no sign of life.

'No injury,' said the mess man confidently, and the other diver nodded. 'We stripped him and can't find anything wrong.'

'What happened?' I asked.

'He fell,' answered the chief officer, who had come into the cabin. 'He was sitting on the rail, foolish man, and started to fall backwards. He would have fallen onto the steel deck of the tug, but I heard the scream and managed to pull him forward so he fell the short distance onto the deck of the tanker.'

'I will look after him,' said the mess man firmly, his normally cheerful face sombre, a very different and assured man from his usual rather subservient self, 'it's important someone is near him when he comes to.'

I was busy, caught up in the preparation for the tow and your inspection, and it was not until just after the tow started – always a tense time – that the mess man reported he was conscious and had managed a drink.

It was some hours later, when the tow had settled down and was behaving well, and the salvage crew were back from pumping out the ballast you had insisted on, that I went to see him.

He was lying on his back covered by a sheet looking at the deck head. His eyes were completely blank, and he made no movement when I called out his name. He appeared completely comatose. The mess man spoke rapidly in Tagaloc, and he turned his head towards where I was standing and said in a toneless voice,

'Sorry Cap, I dead.'

I had no idea what to do, and assumed he must be in shock of some sort, and that I should have sent him ashore. I heard again in my head that awful terrible death cry and thought time would be the healer.

To cut a long story short, with the unceasing care of the mess man who seemed to have grown in stature, he came out of it enough to start work again, but something was missing. When I talked with him, all I could get him to say was, 'sorry Cap, I died. I was dead, but not all of me has come back.'

It was as though a part of his spirit was left on the other side. He was never the same again, some spark of life was gone, snuffed out. It was as though some piece of him was missing, killed off. He was satisfactory in his work; he still dived, but now instead of being a leader he was a follower. He sailed with me for a number of years. His wife left him, I met her and she told me he was so changed that he was not the man she had married, and he never properly recovered. I sent him to a psychiatrist but that did not seem to help. It was as though that death cry really had been a death of sorts, and only part of him returned. Very strange.

* * *

The mariner paused, his eyes closed, his head down, the white goatee beard on his chest, as he thought back.

'It was odd,' he said after a short while, as he lifted his head and continued. 'I had a similar experience when I was a very young man, my first trip as third mate. We were in Port Said waiting for the south bound convoy, and the mail had come on board. I was in my cabin reading a letter from home, when I heard a terrible cry from the captain's cabin on the deck above mine. Not quite the death cry I heard on the tanker, in fact I thought the captain was being murdered. I rushed up to his cabin and found him sitting in his chair, holding a letter in his hand, tears streaming down his face. "Get out," he shouted at me. I was so shocked I said nothing and returned to my cabin, my mind in turmoil, wondering what awful thing had happened.

'He later apologised, and explained that his twenty-year-old son had run down and killed a young boy with his car. He was a different man for the rest of the time I sailed with him, withdrawn and uncommunicative. The cry I heard was from his soul, a soul in torment, knowing his son had ruined his life, but it was a completely different sound from that of the diver on the storage tanker in the Persian Gulf. I've heard the shrieks and screams of men, and women, too, dying in unimaginable pain. Terrible though they were, it was nothing compared with the diver's inhuman cry which froze my soul.'

The mariner was silent, as we absorbed what he had said, the cries of the children playing on the beach so full of life, a rebuke to his story.

7.

Lost

It was a beautiful summer's evening after a hot day, and it was calm in the anchorage entered through a tricky narrow channel. It was high tide so all the dangers were covered and we could only see a mirror-like sea reflecting the bright but dying sunlight.

'Reminds me of a most interesting case in which our friend Richard was involved, God rest his soul,' the lawyer remarked, sweeping his hand around the empty horizon. 'He was placed in a most...' he paused, thinking, and continued, 'well. Let me start from the beginning.'

'If we are going to listen to you for some time I will go below and bring up the bottle and glasses,' said the mariner, standing up from his seat in the cockpit behind the wheel.

'Good idea,' said the naval man, the banker remained silent.

'This is what I remember he told me,' said the lawyer drinking from his glass, 'I turned it into a presentable statement later.'

* * *

I had seen her on the way in and wondered. There was no anchor cable visible, and on checking the chart I realised she was aground. Salvage I thought, no, the bureaucratic Saudis will never give us permission, she will rot away where she is. When permission is finally given to a Saudi she will not be salvable. I was amazed she was there at all, where on earth had she come from.

She was still there on the way back. I was towing the two barges I collected from the port, and what a nightmare that had been, so I did not like to stop. Anyway, I did not have permission. It was hot, Saudi hot, Red Sea summer hot. We passed through the Pearly Gates, one of the hottest places on earth. I was worn out and grateful to be at sea after two weeks of officialdom. The air conditioning was broken down on the tug making the port seem even hotter, airless at night and whenever any wind blew it was filled with dust and sand. However at sea I was under constant tension reef hopping. Still the sunlight was bright, the water clear, and with my lookouts up the mast and forward, I was reasonably confident a reef would be seen before we hit it. The charts were not accurate and there was a warning notice: "navigate with extreme caution."

She slipped out of my mind on arrival, going alongside the casualty, positioning the barges and organising the discharge of the cement onto them. It was hot and I lost a lot of weight working in the holds with the men, humping the bags, cement dust clogging my nostrils and making my skin itch. I had to show willing. My Filipino crew, normally so inventive and keen, were not happy working cargo so I shamed them. Once they started and got going they were cheerful enough and achieved a good rate per hour.

The nights were comparatively cool after the blazing heat of the day, and I suggested we work nights, but they said they preferred to discharge the cement during daylight. The sky was clear, black in the clear unpolluted atmosphere, the stars bright, the pole star low near the northern horizon. I was sitting on the bridge wing of the tug with my last soft drink of the evening, the beer had been sealed in port and I dare not break it until we finally left Saudi waters. My mind was in neutral, just grateful to be here with my salvage than in the harbour, when the thought struck me.

I sat up straight. Did I have the courage to do it? I would be flouting the law, and whatever I felt about Saudi law it was still the law in Saudi waters. Was the possible reward worth the risk, especially as the risk was a Saudi jail and a Saudi jail was to be avoided at all costs for a European? I knew about the Dutch captain who spent a year in jail waiting to be charged for a drink offence, and when he was sentenced to a further year he committed suicide. It was not only the complete lack of privacy which got to many, not that that should matter to anyone who has been to a boarding school in the UK, but also the sense of worthlessness because a prisoner has no rights at all and needs outside help just to eat. Even so, as soon as I formulated the question in my mind I knew it was a stupid question to ask myself because I knew the answer. It was not just the reward, it was the excitement, doing something out of the ordinary, something others would not. I felt that tingling sensation – I knew I was going to do it. I was going to take the risk, I would be living on the edge, and it was not just the risk to myself, as all my crew would be at risk as well. As far as the law was concerned I salved my own conscience. In reality I would be performing a public duty to salve property at risk at sea, and in the environmentally friendly world we now lived in I would be saving the reef from further damage as well. Salvage laws encouraged mariners to save property at sea, and of course there was a duty to save life.

The Chief engineer was sitting in his white shorts, his smooth brown chest wet with sweat in the hot cabin, the porthole open, not to the open sea but the black hull plates of the casualty.

'We leave straight away,' I said.

He looked surprisingly unsurprised and his damp face broke into a smile.

'We wondered how long it would take before you went to have a look,' he said. 'It's that ship?'

I felt deflated after all my soul searching.

'I did not realise I was such an open book,' I laughed.

'We've been running a sweep stake betting on how long it would take you to make up your mind,' he answered, 'a bit longer than many thought,' he chuckled.

'It's a hell of a risk. The Saudis will lock us all up and throw away the key if we are found out.' I said.

'Not with your luck,' he pointed out.

It made me feel uneasy that my crew thought I was lucky, yet humbled they had such faith in me.

'The course is clear of reefs all the way down to her so maximum speed chief,' I said briskly as I left his cabin and made my way to the bridge. Most of the crew seemed to be up so it was only minutes before the lines were let go, and we were at maximum speed heading southwards.

There was no shipping on the run down. We arrived just as the sun was rising above the eastern horizon, bathing the calm sea and surrounding shallows in a sheen of pink, which soon dissipated as the harsh sunlight of summer took over. As soon as the anchor was down the rubber rescue craft, the zed boat was launched.

'You are in command second,' I threw over my shoulder as I left the bridge and ran down to the boat. Arturo, my tough, stocky, strong, intensely keen chief officer was already in the boat along with the two divers and their kit and the two fitters to look after the outboard engine, the spare small engine in its place alongside the big one.

'OK Elmo, take her away, and don't hit anything,' I said to the senior diver who was also a very good small boat driver.

'OK Cap,' he grinned and then spoke rapidly in Tagaloc. The other diver Paquito, surprisingly tall for a Filipino, stood up and moved up to the bow holding onto the painter, his sunglasses firmly in place. The hard-bottomed zed boat was soon planning over the smooth sea towards the ship, looming larger as we closed, accommodation aft and five hatches with cranes forward.

Paquito waved the slow down signal to Elmo and the last few hundred yards were taken very slowly, with Romeo one of the fitters sounding the depth of water with a stick marked in feet, the coral clear in the sunlight. There was sufficient water to circle the ship and see there were no lines or ladders over the side.

Elmo brought the boat alongside amidships and Paquito threw up the grapnel kept on board for just such an eventuality. It hooked onto the rail and he shinned up the rope. Once on deck he lowered the grapnel, the rope ladder was hooked on and we soon had our method of boarding in place.

The deck was covered in rust scale, all paint gone. The white accommodation was dull in the sunlight, the sun seemingly rising fast in the sky, a white orb in the pale blue sky. The ship was completely still and silent. The tug was lying quietly at anchor half a mile away to the north, while in the distance to the south I could see a small attol. I called up the second officer on the tug using our private radio channel, and told him we were going into the accommodation, and to call if he saw anything. I sent the two fitters to sound all the tanks and bilges while the divers were to survey the bottom of the ship.

I crunched my way aft through the rust flakes with Arturo and opened the main door to the accommodation on the port side. There was a musty dead smell, as though the air inside was old. I left the door open as I climbed over the sill and entered, followed by Arturo. We continued aft, opening the cabin doors, looking inside and closing again. They were all empty, the musty smell strong. No one had been here for a long time. There is always an eerie feeling on a dead grounded ship, there is no sound, no movement, no feeling of life as though the heart has been cut out of her. We searched it all, including the mess rooms and galley but found nothing, ending up on the bridge. The chart room table had a thin layer of undisturbed dust on it, otherwise it was as bare and empty as the rest of the ship.

There was absolutely no indication that anyone was aboard, yet I felt uneasy. Why was the ship here, why had no anchor been let go? If no one was here why did I feel so uneasy, almost as though I was being watched. Arturo was completely unconcerned and obviously enjoying himself, and I was glad of his company.

I am very sensitive to atmosphere in enclosed spaces, especially buildings, I can feel if they are happy or unhappy. The most vivid experience I had was house hunting, I was shown a terraced house and as soon as I walked in I knew it was not for me. When I entered the sitting room I told the estate agent something terrible had happened and I could never live there. He pointed to a picture on the wall, a young man sailing his dinghy, full of life and joy. He was killed in a car accident and I must have been feeling something of the parent's terrible grief. It was very strong and I left immediately. I can often tell if a ship is happy or unhappy within seconds of boarding, even though a ship is steel and apparently much more inanimate than bricks and mortar.

I opened the unlocked wheelhouse door and walked out into the fresh, but hot air. The uneasiness did not leave me even though I was outside. There was no one onboard, I told myself, stop being so apprehensive.

'Cap, Cap,' squawked a voice from my radio.

'Yes second,' I replied startled.

'There is a patrol boat about three miles to the north,' he reported, his voice agitated.

My heart sank, and my insides turned to jelly. I looked and could just see a speck near the horizon, he must have identified her through the powerful bridge binoculars on the tug. I felt sick and clenched my buttocks. Fear is a terrible thing if not overcome and I felt frozen, paralysed, like a rabbit in the headlights, the consequences of my action racing through my head, a Saudi jail, not just for me, my people as well. I watched her approaching the tug. I turned as I heard Arturo behind me.

'Seen a ghost,' he laughed.

'No, a Saudi gun boat,' which wiped the smile off of his face.

It broke my fear, enabling me to pull myself together. I called up my tug.

'Has he called up on the VHF?' I asked.

'No Cap.'

'If he does, or comes aboard, and asks what we are doing just tell him we are a salvage company appointed to make a survey and possibly salve the ship. If he asks about permission, just say we have permission from Riyadh.' I instructed.

'OK Cap,' he replied, his voice sounding much calmer.

We watched in silence. The divers and zed boat were on the starboard side or the side away from the gunboat. The awfulness of what I had done, apparently abandoning my salvage, steaming over 90 miles in Saudi waters, all without permission, kept running through my head. All I could do was pray and put on an unconcerned front.

'With your luck, Cap, we will be OK,' said Arturo and he walked back into the wheelhouse.

I continued to watch the patrol boat, my muscles tense, as she drew nearer, a whiff of Arturo's cigarette momentarily breaking my concentration. I recognised her as a Saudi Navy craft as she slowly circled my tug. I could not hear if she was calling on the VHF and the tension was almost unbearable. If they did call, all depended on the second officer, a nice enough fellow and sensible but I did not know how he would respond under this sort of threat. Fear is an irrational thing and takes people in many different ways. I did not know what the Saudi Navy would do if they thought we were there without permission, on the other hand it might not cross the commander's mind that anyone could be so stupid to be there without it. I felt a little better, perhaps that was our saving grace. At the end of the second circle, I thought they must be suspicious, but she made off northwards at speed. My legs almost buckled in relief when I saw her making off.

'Your luck is in again, Cap,' said Arturo's cheerful voice from the wheelhouse. I felt like shouting but held my tongue as I turned around and saw his smiling face in the wheelhouse doorway.

It was now quite hot in the morning sun. I saw the divers come on board and make their way along the deck, and heard the chatter of voices in the wheelhouse, so assumed the fitters had finished their soundings as well. I took a last look round the horizon, empty now except for our tug. It was as though the last half hour of tension and terror never occurred, there was nothing to show for it, a passing incident where nothing had happened. I spoke to the second officer on my radio and the navy boat did not even call up on the VHF. The commander obviously thought we had permission and was not concerned. It was a huge relief and gave me confidence for my future plans.

I went back into the wheelhouse where the divers and fitters were discussing their findings in Tagaloc. They had cleaned off the chart room table and Elmo was finishing off his sketch of the bottom. Romeo was studying the soundings.

'Tanks and bilges all empty,' he reported, his thin face smiling, as he handed me the paper he had been examining, 'looks good.'

'She is only lightly aground,' Elmo informed me holding up his sketch, 'no damage as far as we could see, but we could not get very far underneath.'

It all looked good to me as well. She was apparently tight, the hull was not leaking. I was quite sure we could salve her and tow her to Djibouti. It was whether we could get her out of Saudi waters, but after the gun boat incident I was reasonably confident of this as well. Should I tell the office or not, I wondered. If I told them the world would know once they tried to establish who the owner was and why she was there. No, better to tell no one and just turn up in Djibouti with her. I was not concerned with the past, only the future, and I felt quite excited. My crew obviously thought so as well from their animated discussion, and smiling faces.

'How can we do it, Cap,' asked Arturo, his smooth face beaming, 'do you think we can get away with it?'

'I don't know yet, Arturo,' I answered. 'It is not so much the salvage, it is getting her out of Saudi waters,' I continued, the expectant faces of the divers and fitters fuelling my ambition. 'Anyway, we have to finish the "Rainsland" first and deliver her to port. By then we should have thought of something. Arturo, we will let go of the port anchor, no point letting her drift further onto the reef if there is a high tide and strong wind. It will also enable us to make a quick connection and dispense with the stretcher and forerunner when we come to salve her.'

'Ok Cap, good idea.'

I was still uneasy that I was missing something. I was with other people, and the feeling I was being watched had disappeared, but I still felt uneasy. I decided to set my mind at rest.

'Arturo, I have the most odd feeling we are not alone on board,' I said seriously.

'Ghosts, Cap? I don't think so,' and he laughed, the others laughing with him.

'Ghosts or no ghosts,' I said sharply, 'we will search the whole ship in pairs, open all cupboards, lockers, store rooms everything. Arturo and I will do the accommodation, Romeo you take Enrico and do the engine room and steering flat, Elmo you and Paquito do the deck and forecastle. All of you look for any signs that anyone is or has been onboard recently, food, fire for cooking, clothing, disturbed dust, anything.'

'Ok Cap,' they replied, obviously from their faces thinking I was a bit odd, but quite happy to humour me.

'I am serious, if there is anyone onboard we need to find them. I am quite sensitive to these things, so search thoroughly.'

The others left and I went out onto the port bridge wing where I could see the tug, most reassuring, our escape line. The thought of being marooned on a dead ship in the middle of nowhere in the heat of the Red Sea summer was appalling. I was already sweating. I looked around the horizon, nothing, it was empty, the gun boat long gone, not even a seagull. The sea was calm above the shallows, the coral, with its varied colours, clearly visible.

I stood with my back to the tug and looked at the funnel, the paint dull with age and neglect. I looked further aft and then forward, my eyes moving slowly, taking in every detail. Nothing seemed out of place or stood out in any way. I was in the open, yet I had the uncanny feeling I was not alone, that someone or something was watching me. I walked to the ladder and climbed up onto the monkey island, the deck covered in a layer of dust, undisturbed. There was an almost unrestricted all round view, and I could see the divers entering the forecastle, otherwise nothing had changed, the cranes at the five hatches were stowed, everything looked normal. I looked around the horizon and there was not a thing in sight. The wooden binnacle, its varnish all wasted away leaving dull bare wood, looked quite normal with the two spherical balls and the flinders bar in the middle. I again carefully searched with my eyes the whole ship and again nothing seemed out of place or disturbed in any way, there was no sign of anyone being on board. The sky was cloudless and it was hot with no shade, the sea was calm, the sunlight glinting on it like a reflection from polished stainless steel.

'Ok Arturo,' I said, he had followed me up, 'all looks normal to me, let's go back and search the accommodation.'

'Still think someone's onboard Cap?' his face serious.

'I still have the feeling we are being watched.'

He nodded and followed me down to the bridge deck. He shut the wheelhouse door after we entered, and the chartroom door as we left. There was no sign of anyone or thing in the accommodation.

We found the engine room door, and from the top platform could hear the fitters below. It was cooler and much darker as we made our way down, the only light was from the engine room skylight. I always find a silent engine room slightly unnerving, it is the heart of a ship and silence meant the heart had stopped beating, she was dead. The fitters were looking at the generators, no doubt wondering if they could be started.

'Nothing Cap,' said Romeo, his voice loud in the silent space, 'bilges quite clean and dry, store OK.'

It felt good to be back on deck, even if the sunlight was dazzling at first, and the heat hit us like a blast from a furnace.

'No ghosts,' Arturo said chirpily, grinning, his feet kicking the rust scales as we made our way forward.

I did not reply. The divers were already on the forecastle taking the lashings off the port anchor.

'Everything is OK,' reported Elmo when we arrived, 'shall I let go?'

I nodded.

It only took a few minutes work from my experienced men and the rattle of chain running out shattered the silence, rusty dust filled the air. I watched the anchor splash into the sea followed by the cable. Once the water had settled I could see it lying on the coral, the chain heaped up beside it. The windlass brake was tightened and secured, the devil's claw and locking bar put in place, which would hold the ship if she re-floated. We made our way back to the zed boat secured to the ladder.

Paquito, the last man onboard, lowered the ladder and climbed down the rope they had rigged in a bight. Once he was in the boat Elmo let go of the end of the bight and pulled the rope onboard.

I watched the ship as Elmo slowly drove the boat to deep water, where he opened up the engine to full throttle. There was nothing to indicate we had been on board. The ship grew smaller as the tug grew larger. I was aware my imagination might be playing tricks on me, was I seeing movement where there was none? My people were unconcerned enjoying the rush of apparently cooler air past their sweating faces as the boat picked up speed. I thrust aside all thoughts of "ghosts" as we had found nothing to suggest anyone had been onboard for a long time, and pondered the problem. The hull was apparently sound although the divers had been unable to get under it but the double bottom tanks were empty and the bilges dry. I did not think the actual salvage was a real problem for my tug, it was getting her out of Saudi waters. A salvage permit and clearance were needed, but knowing how the bureaucracy worked it would take many months, if not years and probably be issued to a Saudi. No, I would have to gamble with a Saudi jail, tell no one and sort out any problems in Djibouti. I would then be "salvor in possession" and have negotiating power. The incident with the Saudi Navy gunboat, or rather the non-incident, suggested I had a good chance of getting away with it. The commander obviously thought no one could be brave enough to work in their waters without a permit. My mind was made up.

'Pick up the anchor Arturo,' I ordered, climbing aboard the tug.

'OK Cap,' he replied, walking forward.

'Full ahead back to the Rainsland when the anchor is aweigh, second,' I shouted up to the bridge, 'I am going for a shower.'

'Ok Cap,' he grinned his reply, pleased I was letting him get the tug underway unsupervised.

I heard the engine telegraph ring, the air started engine cough and spring into life, the vibration, he is taking it slowly, I thought, while he turns. I looked out of the shower porthole, the water hot on my back. I could not see the ship, the bow of the tug was swinging to port, the sun was well behind the port beam. He was on track and I felt a little foolish, there was not much he could do wrong unless he deliberately headed for the reef. I heard the telegraph ring again and the engine speed pick up, he is on full speed now, I thought, and turned back into the shower.

'Breakfast, Cap,' suggested Micky, my smiling moon faced mess boy a little later.

'Thanks,' I smiled back as he put down the tray containing a plate of eggs bacon and rice and a mug of tea, the surface shimmering with the vibration of the tug at full speed. I was hungry.

It was an irate Captain I faced when I came alongside the "Rainsland" late in the afternoon.

'Where the devil have you been?" He shouted, his elderly jowls wobbling, red with rage and anger, as I walked into his wheelhouse, cool in the air conditioning.

'On a recce, don't worry it won't delay your re-floating. Why aren't your men working?' I retaliated.

'They wouldn't work without your people,' he replied looking a little shamefaced, the anger and bluster gone as I gave him a look of contempt.

'You should have told me you were going, you are under contract to me. I am going to tell my owners you traipsed off in the middle of the night without permission.' The bluster returning.

I felt like telling him to go to hell and do what he liked, but there was no point antagonising him anymore. It meant an evening session with him listening to his stories I had heard before about an era long gone.

'Don't worry,' I soothed, 'listen, they have started work and we will have discharged enough by tomorrow night which is the highest tide, as you know. The levels are still increasing on my tide gauge.'

'You might have told me,' he grumbled, opening the chartroom door, 'come and have a beer.' His liquor bond had not been sealed by the Saudi customs, not having made the port. He led the way down to his cabin, which took up most of the width of the accommodation and was well appointed with comfortable chairs and a small settee. He even had a proper bath.

My heart sank a little at the prospect of a session and a wasted evening but it was better to keep him on side and worth the effort. Anyway, I thought, there was always a penance to pay for good things, and if I was successful I would be returning to Djibouti with an additional ship in tow.

The next night we were successful and re-floated the "Rainsland." She was anchored clear of the reef. The reloading of the cement from the barges took three days and the divers reported the bottom was scratched and indented but had no cracks or holes. I had previously surveyed the channel and marked it with buoys anchored on the shallow patches. I was able to lead the "Rainsland" which was under her own power clear of the reef area with the empty barges secured alongside my tug. She anchored outside the port to await a berth while I went inside.

It was a happy fat elderly captain who signed my termination letter when I came alongside having delivered the barges back into the port and obtained my port clearance.

'Thank you Captain,' he said. 'You and your people did a good job. I won't mention your unexplained disappearance,' he smiled, 'you are lucky, it must be exciting running around with your tug.'

'It has its moments,' I laughed. 'Well good luck, and enjoy your stay in Saudi.'

He looked sad as I left his bridge, perhaps remembering his lost youth. How had he ended up on an elderly ship carrying cement at the end of his life rather than a modern container ship to crown his career. I was itching to get away and salve my "lost" ship.

She was still in the same place, no sign of movement, when I boarded the next morning. It seemed odd I found not a single piece of paper on board, and her name was painted out on the bow and stern. Normally there is something, a log book, old publications, but there was nothing. Someone for whatever reason had removed everything. I planned with Arturo, after we left the port, what we would do to minimise the time we were engaged in illegal activity.

It was a beautiful morning, not a cloud in the sky, the sea was smooth and shining like ice reflecting the sunlight, but it was already hot. I anchored the tug as close as I dared, just a couple of feet under the keel. I knew the state of tide from my observations of the last few weeks and knew it was rising. I expected to be ready by high water.

The metal work boat and zed boat towed the main tow wire, with barrels made fast every hundred feet or so to keep it off the coral. The divers made fast a wire strop just above the anchor shackle and through that a longer strop to which the main tow wire was shackled. I was dispensing with the nylon stretcher and forerunner, I would have sufficient catenary with the weight of the chain, and it would do the work of the stretcher. Essentially it was a fast method of making a connection, and speed was essential. The quicker I got out of Saudi waters the happier I would be.

Arturo and his men were on the forecastle putting additional wire lashings onto the chain. A lot of weight would come in it when we tried to re-float. The men were sweating in the mid-morning heat, their heads swathed in towels, bodies fully covered, hurrying to be ready for high tide. There was a container of cool water they had brought with them and I helped myself.

'I am going to the bridge for a final check and look around,' I said. Arturo nodded.

I climbed down the ladder onto the main deck and crunched my way aft on the rust scale, my eyes constantly moving, checking to see if anything was out of place, or would move once we were out into the Red Sea, if we were successful.

I entered the accommodation, cooler than in the bright sunlight, but hot without air-conditioning, still stuffy and musty. I made my way up to the bridge to check on the navigation lights rigged by the electrician, I was going to comply with all international regulations. That feeling of unease was with me again on the bridge, this time I was alone and it was quite strong. Arturo laughed it away before, but he was not here this time.

I leaned with my middle pressed against the chart room table and looked out over the top of the panel, through the wheelhouse window. I could just see the sea, still calm, sparkling in the sunlight, but not the men working on the forecastle.

The feeling of unease intensified and I reached for my radio when I heard a sound. The hairs on the back of my neck arose in alarm and I felt a stab of fear, I was momentarily frozen. My imagination ran riot with imagined horrors even though it was daylight, it was like a bad nightmare. I turned towards the sound and saw a figure framed in the wheelhouse door window, long black hair, lengthy black beard and piercing black eyes under bushy eyebrows. The door opened, the sound breaking my fear. An almost naked figure moved in and a voice croaked.

'Hullo, my name is Nigel Newton.'

I was almost as shocked by the voice as by the bearded wild looking creature, educated and English. His body was quite hairy and tanned dark, in fact if it was not for the voice I would have taken him for an Indian. He was incredibly thin, his ribcage clearly visible, his legs thin and long like his toes, bare on the wooden deck, a ragged loin cloth around his waist. He held out his hand as he shuffled towards me, his fingers long and slender. His black hair hung past his shoulders and the beard reached his chest. He was about my height, almost six foot.

'I am an Englishman,' he said clearing his voice, 'I have not spoken to anyone for many months.'

My animal fear had disappeared as I realised he was no physical threat to me. My feelings of unease were fully justified I thought and wondered what incredible circumstances brought an Englishman to be on board a "lost" ship aground in the wastes of Saudi reefs miles from any sort of civilization, and looking as though he was almost starving.

'What on earth are you doing here?' I rather stupidly asked.

'I am a fugitive from the Saudi police and I need your help,' he said, his voicing sounding stronger.

'How long have you been onboard?'

'About a year.'

'A year, good God,' I expostulated, wondering if I was talking to a mad man, but he sounded quite sane.

'I escaped from a Saudi jail and managed to get on board when the ship was in Jeddah waiting for the tow. She was there a long time.'

'A Saudi jail, you escaped? I don't believe you,' I said, shocked. 'No one escapes from a Saudi jail, least of all a European, even if you do look like a local.'

'I've been training myself to look like that and I speak fluent Arabic.'

'How long has the ship been here?'

'About three months. She broke adrift from the tug in a storm and ended up here.'

'And no one came to tow her away?' I asked, surprised.

'Some Dutchmen turned up in a tug, had a look around but never came back.'

'Why didn't you go with them?'

'I didn't think they would help, I thought they would turn me in,' he shook his head, his beard sweeping his bare torso.

'Which is what I should do. Where have you been hiding?'

'In the funnel.'

'Well, well, no wonder I felt uneasy on the bridge. Food?' I asked.

'Raw fish and whatever I could find. I did not dare to light a fire and cook.'

The whole thing was surreal, and what was I going to do? Stowaways were a real problem, no one wanted them, and an escaped convict too.

'You must help me, you are my last chance. I shall go mad staying here any longer, especially as I have seen and spoken, you have broken my solitude,' he made it sound like an accusation.

'Help you, what do you mean?' I asked sharply.

'You must smuggle me out of Saudi,' he said quite firmly.

'You must be joking, I will hand you over to the Saudi authorities,' I replied sharply.

'No no that will be a death sentence,' he shouted.

'What were you in jail for?'

'I killed someone. It was self defence but the police did not believe me, nor did the court. I am also charged with being a terrorist.'

'A murderer, a terrorist,' I breathed, aghast.

'I was waiting for the appeal when I escaped. You must help me,' he pleaded. 'You must trust me, it was self defence I promise. You have my word as an Englishman.'

'There is not much time, I am going to re-float this ship and tow her to Djibouti,' I said.

He stood up straight and his thin lips smiled through the beard.

'Problem solved, just take me to Djibouti,' he sounded relieved.

'As an illegal immigrant, people smuggling is a serious offence in today's world. You say you have been convicted a terrorist too, it's almost worse than murder, aiding and abetting a terrorist. It will land me and my people in jail as well. God what a mess,' I retorted.

It then struck me. I could not hand him over, I would be incriminating myself. In the eyes of the Saudis I was engaged in an illegal activity, stealing a ship and towing her away. If I took him to the port they would arrest me for boarding the ship without a permit. I was supposed to leave Saudi waters as soon as the port clearance was issued. I was quite happy I was doing the right thing salving the ship and saving the reef from further damage even if a little unorthodox, I was even performing a public duty, but the Saudis would not see it like that.

He moved closer to me, his smell quite strong, took hold of my shoulder and looked me in the eye.

'You have got to believe me, I am not a murderer, it was in self defence and I am not a terrorist,' he said earnestly.

'Why should I believe you?'

'Because I told you the truth. I could have made up some story, but I told you the truth, why would I make up something so damning?'

'Presumably because I would have found out in Djibouti.'

'You've got to trust me. I am an Englishman and I give you my word,' he repeated. 'Take me to Djibouti, no one need know I am onboard except you, I will go back into the funnel.'

'And what do you do in Djibouti?'

'You arrange a flight and I fly to Paris.'

I laughed rather wildly. 'What do I tell the immigration authorities? I could certainly forget about you and let you swim ashore.'

'But the only way back to Europe is by air, and for that I need to have entered Djibouti legally,' he said.

'Correct. However you need a passport.'

'I have a passport.'

I did not know what to think, escaping from a Saudi jail was unheard of and they would have confiscated his passport.

'Let's see.'

He put his hand inside his loincloth and pulled out the familiar burgundy coloured document. He handed it to me and I opened it. It all looked in order and in date as well, occupation consultant which covered a multitude of sins. I realised it was quite possible to pull this off. All I had to do was put him on the tug's crew list and with a valid passport he would be entered into Djibouti. The agent would have no reason to question his presence, I would say he was a consultant if asked, and could book him a flight. It really was too easy, unless they knew about his alleged crime which I doubted. What about my crew, I thought. If I briefed Arturo I was quite certain they would say nothing to the authorities, and anyway, they knew nothing of the killing. It was all down to trust, if I believed him then I felt morally bound to help him. The Saudi judicial system was not the same as ours and justice was an intellectual exercise rather than reality. As far as I was concerned there would be no justice, tangle in any way with the Saudis and you were guilty even if you had done nothing illegal. However if anything went wrong in Djibouti I would be in deep trouble, and even the French would not help me if it turned out he really was a terrorist.

'You realise it would be easier just to leave you there on that tiny piece of coral which shows at low water,' I pointed out.

'But that would be murder,' he said shocked.

'No, once out at sea I would radio the authorities and tell them where you were.'

'That would still be murder because they will execute me, not so much for the alleged crimes but because I escaped.'

'Not in my book.' I said looking him in the eye. 'For all intents and purposes I am the law here as far as you are concerned. Your presence is putting me and my people at risk and they are my first responsibility. My crew will do as I tell them and you have no one else to turn to in this wasteland.'

'You have to believe me, you have to trust me,' he cried.

'I agree it is all about trust, do I trust you, do I believe you? Your story is so incredible. I certainly believe you are a fugitive, but if I don't turn you in here maybe I should turn you in at Djibouti.'

I looked at him while my mind was racing. I could not turn him in here, not that he knew, but I could in Djibouti. I made up my mind as my radio burst into life.

'Cap, you OK, we are waiting for you, all is ready.'

'Coming Arturo,' I replied watching Nigel's face.

'Right, go back into your funnel. I won't turn you in here, you can stay on board for the tow down to Djibouti. I will come across in the zed boat once out of Saudi waters and tell you of my decision. Presumably you have water, what about food. Looks as though you could do with a decent meal.'

'I have water and some dried fish so will not starve.' He smiled, 'thank you,' he said quietly, 'I won't let you down, trust me, I am an Englishman.'

I left the bridge and quickly went down to the boat. The ladder was rigged and I climbed down followed by Arturo who had not said a word. The work boat was already back at the tug and out of the water. Elmo drove fast and I jumped out as soon as he put her alongside.

'Tell the bosun to heave up the anchor Arturo. Take the re-floating party over straight away.'

I went onto the bridge. The tug was facing the same way as the casualty. The electrician was manning the tow winch answering my call on the telephone. Once the anchor was off the bottom, I put the telegraph on slow ahead and ordered the helmsman hard a port. I went onto the monkey island so I could see the tow wire which was moving across the stern.

'Midships, steer north,' I shouted down to the second officer standing on the bridge wing. The tow wire was leading aft. I looked through my binoculars and could see the chain was beginning to straighten out; the anchor would be dragging over the coral.

'Half ahead,' I shouted down and a little later, 'full ahead.'

The tow wire was beginning to sing and the chain was tight. I could see the bottom of the anchor shank where the strop was passed through the shackle. The ship had not moved. My heart sank, it was almost high water. The zed boat was returning from dropping the three men. I went back down to the bridge and called up the riding crew on the radio.

'Any sign of movement Arturo?'

'Negative Cap. We are greasing the chain in the hawse pipe.'

'Good. Let me know as soon as there is any movement.'

I went hard a port and the tug started moving sideways through the water towards the shallow waters, the coral. I went over as far as I dared, the echo sounder showing just a few feet under the keel. I went hard a starboard, and the tug pivoted on the tow wire and started moving back away from the coral. I could see the anchor lift part out of the water as the extra weight of the tug came onto the wire.

'She's moving Cap,' said Arturo's voice from the radio, unusually excited.

I saw the bow begin to swing towards the tug and went into the wheelhouse.

'Steer north,' I told the helmsman.

I went back to the wing to watch the casualty, the sun bright ahead, high in the sky. The bow continued to swing and then it was pointing at the stern of the tug, the tow wire out of the water, bar taught.

'She's coming Cap,' Arturo's voice calmer now out of the radio.

I looked over the side and saw the tug beginning to make way ahead through the water. Done it, I thought with elation.

'Tell the fitters to sound round the tanks and bilges. I will stop to let the divers take a look at the bottom,' I told Arturo on the radio.

'Ok Cap.'

It was worth the risk of staying an extra half hour or so to check. If we had damaged the bottom, now was the time to patch it before we were out in the Red Sea. It seemed a long wait while we drifted clear of the shallows and I pondered the problem of Nigel. I still did not know if I trusted him, even though he was an Englishman.

'All Ok Cap, we are coming back,' said Arturo's now usual calm voice on the radio.

As soon as the Zed boat was out of the water I started towing, building up to full speed. In the calm waters inside the reefs we were soon making a respectable seven knots. Even if we did see any patrol boats I doubted they would stop me, it would all seem perfectly normal, a tug towing a ship, and I had hoisted the towing diamond, the daylight towing signal. Arturo came onto the bridge.

'We should be out through the Pearly Gates at dusk tonight,' I said.

'I hope we all pass through,' he giggled, a practicing Catholic.

'We have a serious problem.' I had thought very carefully about involving the crew, but I did not see how I could get Nigel into Djibouti without them knowing. Without the means to get out of Djibouti he would be stuck, and if picked up we all would be implicated. No, if I was going to help I would have to do it properly, and that meant putting him on the crew list and clearing him in. Did I trust him; I suppose I answered my own question by telling Arturo. Once I told him the die was cast.

'There is a man on board our casualty,' I said quietly.

'A man,' he said shocked. 'You mean your ghost was real.'

'Yes. He is an Englishman, he is in the funnel. I am going to put him on the crew list and help him get out of Djibouti. The less you know the less you can tell.'

'If it is OK by you it is OK by us,' he said quietly.

'Thanks Arturo. I don't think it will be a problem, immigration won't have any reason to question him if he is on the crew list and his passport is in order. Once we are through the Pearly Gates I will go across and bring

121

him back, Mickey can cut his hair and clean him up, he looks like some wild man from Borneo.'

'Tell the crew, if anyone should ask, that he is a consultant we had for our salvage of the "Rainsland," but they should not talk about him to anyone.'

'Ok Cap.'

It was dark when I went across in the zed boat, the stars bright, a slight swell running and the tug at slow speed. The second officer and Elmo were with me as I made my way onto the bridge and out onto the wing, where Nigel was standing.

'Ok we will take you back to the tug,' I said, 'I will help you get out of Djibouti.'

'He stepped forward and hugged me, his body shaking with dry sobs, his beard rough against my face. I gently pushed him away.

'Pull yourself together; I have two of my people with me,' I said.

'It's been so long,' he sobbed.

'Got your passport, that is all that matters.'

'Yes,' he said handing it to me his hand shaking.

'Anything else?'

'No.'

More than a year onboard with nothing, not even a book to read, I thought, no wonder he is a bit emotional. The navigation lights were working satisfactorily, powered by the batteries the electrician had put on board. I looked ahead and could see the white towing light on the tug, the bright deck lights almost obscuring it.

I waited with Nigel, who was now in control of himself, at the ladder while Arturo went forward to check the chain.

'Are you strong enough to climb down the rope ladder?'

'Yes,' he replied, 'I may be skinny but I am OK.'

Back on the tug I handed him over to Mickey, my versatile mess man.

'What a transformation, you look quite civilised,' I said when he came into my cabin sometime later, short hair and a trimmed beard.

'Thank you for all your help and trust in me,' he said.

We talked for a long time, about UK, his school, family, and I felt my trust was not misguided and I was doing the right thing. It all worked out as I thought. The immigration said nothing; the agent did not raise any questions and booked him on the Paris flight out of Djibouti. I doubted if head office would even pick up the extra air fare.

The office was pleased with my coup, finding and salving the ship. However, they were not so pleased I said nothing until arrival Djibouti. It turned out the underwriter had already paid out two total losses and did not want to know. We sold her to Karachi and my tug towed her to the breakers beach while I flew back to Singapore. The incident faded from my mind as more urgent problems presented themselves to be solved. I did notice a little item in Lloyd's list stating that a decomposed body had been discovered in a double bottom when they cut up the ship. I did not think too much about it at the time.

It was many months later when I received a letter postmarked Djibouti. I wondered who on earth was writing to me from there. Inside was an envelope post-marked Paris. I opened it and found a picture postcard of a cathedral in Paris, and written on it were the words,

'I did not kill the man in the tank, merely assumed his identity.' It was unsigned.

I sat down in shock, the item in Lloyds List leaped into my mind. Had my trust been betrayed and he was not who he said he was, or his passport showed?

* * *

The lawyer finished picking up his glass. The sun was setting, a fiery red bathing the rocks uncovered by the falling tide in colour. It was calm, the only sound occasional gurgle from the swiftly flowing tide. The silence was broken by the banker.

'So, our friend aided and abetted a convicted criminal and terrorist.'

'We don't know that,' rebuked the lawyer 'although Richard broke numerous laws taking him into Djibouti, apart from defrauding his owners of the air fare as well. However were his actions justified, saving an Englishman from certain death in Saudi? They behead you there.'

'With the information he had I think I would have done the same,' said the mariner.

'You and he were always a soft touch under your tough exteriors,' scoffed the banker.

'As I lawyer I could not have done it, as a man I don't know.'

'Interesting,' said the navy man, picking up the empty bottle and glasses. He went below, followed by the others.

8.

Mistake

It is one of the most beautiful anchorages on the south coast. We were sitting in the cockpit, well pleased with ourselves having anchored under sail.

'A neat manoeuvre,' commented a cheerful mariner, stroking his white goatee beard.

'Not too bad, for our more mature years,' said the naval man.

'Hope the windlass works. Don't fancy weighing the anchor by hand,' grunted the banker.

We had drifted in on the dying evening breeze, on a lovely summer evening and it was now quite hot.

'That oil rig ashore reminds me of the Gulf,' remarked the lawyer, 'and the end of Richard and his company.'

A little later, with the inevitable bottle on the varnished table, glinting in the last of the sunlight, the lawyer was in a rather sombre mood, his dry toneless voice quite quiet as the stillness resumed.

'Yes, it was sad in a way but he had the chance to get out when on top. Well, near the top. His company was in terminal decline, the new owners destroying it.'

'It was before I really got to know him,' put in the mariner, 'although I had met him professionally.'

'It was the death of Adrian, his protégé, that started what I might call the rot. He did not own the company, although he owned shares. He never envisaged the old man selling out, which is what he did, and quite suddenly too.

'It clipped his wings. The loss of some of his people in Iranian waters, the sinking of one of his tugs hit by an Iraqi missile and death of more crew, shortly after the old man sold out, finished him off. I think he lost heart, after all he was a civilian.

'He had salved three loaded super tankers in a short space of time, and the company was rich, but it all turned sour. He resigned, purchased a sailing yacht and sailed round the world.'

'That is when I got to know him and his crew,' put in the mariner, refilling his glass.

The setting sun was hidden by the magnificent scenery stretching for miles, the only sign of human habitation being the house at the end of the short peninsula and the rig partly hidden by the trees, the whole bathed in a light pink.

'The story does not end there,' continued the lawyer, a little frostily at the interruption. 'Richard was out of salvage for good, but the team he had built up were not. He recruited a very live wire salvage man, Paul, who blossomed and grew under Richard's tutelage, a very different person from Adrian, not so pleasant but very effective all the same.

'Paul took the bull by the horns, collected up his team and decamped from Singapore to the Emirates, leaving the company which was in receivership due to the bankruptcy of the holding company. Although he succeeded in putting a syndicate together to purchase the salvage company he was stymied in his efforts. Politics I believe. A potential buyer from the Middle East was disappointed in not being able to buy, and so bought the people instead. He'd offered Paul the chance to set up a new division in the buyer's existing company and use the tugs and equipment to take advantage of the tanker war raging in the Gulf.

'Paul, being an opportunist, seized the opportunity with both hands and persuaded key people to join him. It was the opportunity of a lifetime.

'The reality in Sharjah was rather different from the picture painted by the continental, the Middle Eastern buyer's front man, but Paul had broken his bridges, and he had to make do with what he found. He could not return to Singapore. The team he brought with him were enthusiastic, and any disappointment was soon dissipated by action, and lots of it.

'I, as you know, had been the lawyer to Richard's company, and Paul, whom I knew from taking his evidence on various salvage cases, asked me to be his lawyer. I agreed. Even at my more advanced years, it was exciting to be involved, with what in reality was a new salvage company. We planned our campaign very carefully to be recognised as a professional salvage company from the very beginning, and they performed well enough for this to be achieved.

'Paul was based in Sharjah and was the anchor man ashore, liaising as necessary with the owner and his front man, but that does not concern us here. Paul ran the salvage from obtaining the Lloyd's Open Form to arbitration in London. They had a couple of good salvage jobs under their belt, and I got to know Simon the master of the newly acquired salvage tug, the "Eagle" ex "Titan" from Europe. He was a serious young man of medium height, quite self-effacing until one saw him on his tug when it was totally clear who was in command.

'The "Eagle" was quite old but well maintained and fitted with modern salvage equipment, in particular fire-fighting. This salvage was a little different, and for once did not involve a tanker. This is Simon's story.'

* * *

We were on salvage station off Sharjah, drifting with the wind and tide. It was a fine night and very pleasant, although we were always on alert. The war at sea had increased in intensity considerably, with both Iraq and

Iran attacking ships, quite indiscriminately, with what at times appeared to be a deliberate policy to kill and maim seafarers.

It took a conscious mental effort to distance oneself from the feeling we were a target, but were there to help and assist others. The longer one stayed at sea in the Gulf, the easier that came to be.

I was listening to VHF. Channel 16, the distress channel, when I heard a ship, whose name I did not quite catch, reporting he could see a ship on fire off of Jebel Ali, the main port for Dubai.

I immediately rang half ahead, and then full ahead on the engine telegraph. She was an old fashioned but good vessel without bridge control, and once she was moving I instructed the man on the wheel to steer south westwards towards Jebel Ali. Meanwhile, I called up the vessel which made the report, and eventually obtained the approximate position of the distress. The casualty herself had not made any May Day or SOS call, so I assumed she was hit on the bridge, which would have destroyed her communications. The "Eagle" was up to her maximum speed, when the chief engineer holding his usual cleaning rag, boiler suit open to his navel, arrived on the bridge.

'Casualty on fire off of Jebel Ali chief,' I said calmly, although I was bursting with excitement with the need to be there first, 'can you squeeze any more out of her? We must beat the competition.'

He grunted and quickly left the bridge, a man of few words, but Duncan was a brilliant engineer and a fantastic person to have on a salvage.

A little later, there was a marked increase in speed, the whole tug vibrating under the thrust of her powerful propeller. There was nothing I could do until we were up to the casualty. I posted a lookout in the crow's nest, and it was not long before he reported sighting the ship on fire. I climbed up onto the monkey island above the bridge to have a look, leaving Chen the chief officer in charge on the bridge.

It appeared the casualty was on fire aft and it was soon apparent the accommodation was alight, lighting up the sky for miles around. The fore part of the ship was unaffected.

Pepe the bosun had been busy. When I manoeuvred the "Eagle" alongside the burning casualty, the small Yokohama fenders were ready on the starboard side, all the hoses and fire equipment were laid out on the aft deck, and the fire monitor was manned and throwing its 650 tonnes per hour of water far ahead of the tug.

I put the "Eagle" starboard side to the starboard side of the casualty in the 69 position, that is, the stern of the tug to the bow of the ship. The water from the fire monitor engulfed the accommodation, while my crew ran out the hoses and fought the fire from the main deck. The flames shooting high above the bridge and flashing out of portholes were soon doused without the use of foam, and the crew entered the accommodation to put out the pockets of fire still burning.

An opposition tug arrived on the scene and started spraying the accommodation with water. I firmly pointed out over the radio that I was the salvor in possession, the main fire was out and my crew were inside the accommodation. He should move off and avoid injuring my crew.

I told a Reynaldo, the radio officer, to send a telex to Paul suggesting he phoned the tug owners and tell them to pull off their tug before our people were injured.

The crew of the casualty, the "Freedom Explorer," had been sheltering on the forecastle, but when they saw the flames reducing came on board the tug. The captain, a large and voluble Greek was very grateful.

'Thank you, thank you, Captain for saving us,' he gushed kissing me on both cheeks, his breath suggesting he had been eating something strong. 'We were attacked by two helicopters,' he continued excitedly, 'a parachute bomb was dropped on the monkey island, which set the bridge on fire and killed the third officer and quartermaster, a missile or rocket went directly into the accommodation, passing through the chief engineer's cabin, who is still missing and out the other side.

Another missile went into the engine room, but has not exploded. A third helicopter arrived on the scene and the two attacking ones flew off in the direction of Iran.'

'Okay, thanks Captain,' I said, 'there is a bit of paperwork. If you would sign my Lloyds Open Form, please.'

He looked at it, then walked to the wheelhouse window and looked at his ship. There were still pockets of fire glowing in the porthole windows. He returned to the chart table and asked gruffly, 'commission for me if I sign.'

'Commission,' I replied sharply, shocked, 'I have just put out the fire on your ship, Captain, risked my tug and the lives of my crew to save you and you ask for a commission. If you don't sign I shall initiate a court case claiming salvage. It is much easier for your owners to work with us on LOF.'

'Okay okay, I sign,' he said hastily.

It was not the first time I have been asked for a commission, but the last time was in
very different circumstances.

I informed the opposition tug which was still hanging around, and sent a message to Paul, who no doubt would pressurise the owners to remove their tug.

It was now early morning, still dark, and there was no sign of fire only the torch lights of our crew showing in the portholes. The corpse of the chief engineer, who had been hit by the missile, or rather his remains, were put in a body bag. The charred remains of the two killed on the bridge were collected and put into another bag. I was much more affected by death than my crew, who had a very healthy attitude towards it.

I thought things were settling down nicely, and was about to instruct Chen to connect up the tow, when we heard the unmistakable clatter and chatter of an approaching helicopter.

The captain of the "Freedom Explorer" was with me on the bridge and became very agitated. Some of his crew were on the casualty looking for their personal effects, but the accommodation was gutted. He shouted to his men to get out.

'It will attack again,' he shouted, waving his arms in the air.

I sounded the fire alarm switching on the bells, and continually sounded the whistle. Everyone ran out of the accommodation to see what the matter was. We frantically shouted at them and indicated they should run forward as the helicopter loomed overhead. It was not showing any lights. We heard the whoosh of a rocket, and it entered halfway up the accommodation and exploded.

I desperately sent May Days on the VHF channel 16, my hand holding the radio microphone shaking, while Reynaldo sent SOS on the distress frequencies.

The fire monitor on the mast was restarted, and one of the crew played it over the accommodation. Chen rallied the people on the deck of the casualty and aimed the hoses through the broken portholes.

The helicopter hovered almost overhead, and I was tense with fear, thinking it might rocket-attack the tug clearly visible with all the deck lights shining brightly. The poor captain had thrown himself on the deck, but I realised if the tug was attacked it made no difference if I was standing or lying down.

We heard the whoosh of a second rocket but it must have been a bad shot, because it did not hit anything and disappeared into the night.

The sound of a second helicopter approaching increased our alarm and fear, but this one had flashing lights and the one overhead, moved off.

'Load a portable fire pump and connect up. We must get out of here as quickly as possible and tow to Jebel Ali,' I shouted at Chen who had forgotten his radio.

'Okay Captain,' he shouted back from his position in front of the accommodation.

This was the first time an attack had taken place so close to Dubai and the first time there had been a second attack. I thought if we could get the casualty into port we would be safe.

My salvage crew worked wonders and within half an hour, I was moving the tug off the casualty and turning to commence the tow to Jebel Ali.

The unwelcome and frightening sound of yet another helicopter approaching was heard, but I was too busy to be afraid. The Greek threw himself down onto the deck. I blew the whistle to alert those in the accommodation.

I now had the tug ahead of the "Freedom Explorer" and was starting to tow. We then saw the helicopter with flashing lights approach, and the darkened one left without firing. I felt almost dizzy with relief. This was unheard of a third attack.

Speed was quickly built up and as dawn was beginning to illuminate the port I entered with the assistance of the harbour tugs. Paul had worked his usual miracles in arranging and obtaining permission. He was waiting at the berth and came on board from a linesman's boat as I went alongside the casualty to provide services.

'Well done,' he congratulated me, shaking my hand, his face wreathed in smiles. He turned to commiserate with the Greek captain.

'We must search for any unexploded ordnance,' he said laughing. 'I was economical with the truth when I arranged with the harbourmaster to bring you in.'

We entered the still warm and dripping accommodation. All the fires were out, and nothing was found. However, it was another matter in the engine room. There was something in the forecastle, reported Pepe, who had gone forward. We followed him, and in the gloom Pepe shone his torch onto a metal case which had been hidden among the spare ropes.

'Don't touch,' I urged. It appeared to be a wireless.

'Get the captain,' I ordered and a crew member went out. We continued to look at the object until joined shortly afterwards by the Greek.

'Don't know,' he retorted to our question, appearing quite shocked.

We sealed the forecastle and returned to the tug, while Paul went ashore and drove off in his car. It was not long before he was back with two uniformed officers. I went back to the ship where the officers inspected the box.

'Homing device', they reported.

'Homing device,' queried Paul.

'It sends out a signal on a predetermined frequency, which presumably the helicopters can tune into.'

'Never heard of this before, must be some reason,' I asked.

'Well it is harmless now, because I have switched it off,' said one of the officers.

'We will take it ashore.'

We wondered if the owners had done a deal with the Iranians, unworthy thought though it was, concluded Simon.

* * *

The lawyer continued, 'No one discovered why the device had been placed on board or who had done it. Obviously someone wanted the ship attacked, but the owners persuaded the insurance investigators that they had nothing to do with it. It was not in their interests, because they had a profitable charter for their ship, now lost due to the attack. Lloyds promptly paid the total loss.

'The military kept quiet and said not a word, although they removed the unexploded ordnance in the engine room. Paul got told off for misinformation.

'And that was that, Paul and his people got a good salvage award, although low values, and the matter was forgotten.'

'Must have been a mistake on the part of whoever placed it on board with a low value cargo like that,' remarked the mariner.

'I wonder what the military found out,' mused the navy man. 'They would have a good chance of finding out where the device came from. It was must have been the Iranians because they were the only ones to use helicopters for attacking ships.'

'It has remained a mystery to this day, a footnote in the history of war,' said the lawyer.

'The Iranians must have been after an Iraqi cargo but got the wrong ship,' said the banker as they went below, leaving the peaceful scene, the rig visible in the moonlight.

9.

Naru

The sun was out and it was hot for these waters. The yacht was anchored off the beach in an open roadstead, fair weather only, but the forecast was good. Shrieks of joy could be heard from the children playing and splashing in the water, their parents watching from the dry sand higher up. The cockpit awning was rigged to shield us from the hot sun sinking slowly in the west and the tea things were spread on the varnished table.

'Reminds me of fine weather in the east,' remarked the mariner, stroking his goatee beard very white in the afternoon sun shine.

'Too hot for me,' grumbled the banker from under his wide brimmed panama hat. The navy man and lawyer remained silent, wondering what the mariner was going to say next.

'It was in Richard's early days with an old-fashioned tug, two engines coupled to a single propellor shaft, but she was big for her day, although rather low horse power. The Messina was his first command, and he was very proud of her, perhaps even in love as much as a man can be with an inanimate object. He was a natural ship handler, and despite her un-manoeuvrability he could almost make her dance. They were in Hong Kong on salvage standby, and I think had been there some time. It was summer and hot during the typhoon season. They had arrived in Hong Kong, running free from Japan, at the beginning of July just after typhoon Ruby. Three weeks later, a tropical storm passed over, it blew hard with lots of rain, but nothing dramatic happened.

'It was on a day not unlike of this one, when I met him in the Pacific on his yacht, anchored in an atoll. It had a difficult entrance, and he had watched with interest to see if I hit any of the unmarked reefs. He came on board for drinks, which extended to supper, and this story sitting in the cockpit, the bimini lowered so we could admire the Southern Hemisphere sky so much clearer than our northern one. I felt it was possible to reach out and touch the stars they shone so brightly. This is what he told me with his eyes closed, his rather sombre face animated as though reliving a life-long past.'

* * *

I had been in command for just over a year and we were in Hong Kong during the typhoon season on salvage standby. Earlier in the year we had picked up a ship with engine trouble in the South China Sea and towed her to Japan, but that had been a towage contract not salvage. It was salvage which interested me. After a couple of weeks in Shimonoseki it had been decided to spend the typhoon season in Hong. We had been there some time and I was glad to get instructions to proceed at economical speed to Sandakan, Sabah on the north east coast of Borneo. The message did not say why, and although I had an open dated port clearance I decided to leave the next morning. It gave the crew time to say goodbye to the various friends they had made during our rather prolonged stay, there was a significant Filipino population in the colony, and pay off the Mama San who had been alongside in her small junk with the girls.

It was summer and hot. A tropical storm had passed close by, but nothing much happened, no ships in trouble, just a few people injured, that was all. In those days pilotage was not compulsory, and I always did my own, which was very satisfying.

We left early in the morning, the sun rising over the outlying islands, and once clear of their shelter the residual swell made the tug pitch and roll. However, the weather was fine and balmy and we ambled down towards Borneo, at our economical speed on one engine. It was very pleasant sitting on the bridge, my refreshment hot or cold depending on the time of day, secured in its holder, welded to the bridge wing. The welder was a most useful man to have on board. The crew were happy to be leaving Hong Kong having spent all their money although the bosun and mess man were almost late on board, I was picking up the anchor when they arrived.

I looked at the chart as usual checking the positions put on by the officer of the watch, at this time Juanito, my handsome new third officer who was desperately trying to prove himself. I realised if I slowed down slightly and altered course I could have a look at Scarborough Reef, which was almost on the way in the South China Sea.

I always wanted to see it ever since being on the Borneo run with the log carriers. The timing was perfect. I would take morning stars with the chief officer Edgar, and knowing our position would easily find the reef, which I knew from the pilot book was big but low-lying and not easily picked up by radar.

So this is what I did, after discussing it with Edgar. We found the reef just after daylight, an old wreck giving a good echo. I crept in on the lee side, although there was not much wind. I went in as far as I dared, the echo sounder running and anchored on the edge of it close by shallow water, the coral occasionally showing. I took the rubber boat away with the divers and discovered the entrance to the lagoon. We took a few soundings as I thought it might be useful knowledge for the future.

The crew spent the morning bathing, those who wanted to, the rest fishing, and the divers captured crayfish. A most enjoyable time was had by all and I had a magnificent crustacean lunch washed down with a Berry Bros white wine. An engine repair was logged to account for the time spent at the reef.

* * *

'Naughty boy,' commented the lawyer, 'falsifying the logbook.' The navy man laughed as if the practice was not completely unknown.

'Being economical with the truth,' laughed the banker. Quite an unusual event for him, laughing, being of serious nature.

'Sailing a little close to the wind,' said the mariner, 'he could hardly tell the office he'd stopped at the reef for a bathing party and crayfish catching, omission is better than alteration.' He laughed and continued.

* * *

We completed the rest of the voyage safely, passing through the Mindoro passage which separates Borneo from the Philippines and across the Sulu Sea to Sandakan. It was a bit of a one-eyed place, but I knew it well from my log carrying days. I went alongside the jetty, which was empty. The agent came on board, a tall Englishman dressed in smart whites wearing a sun hat over his rather thin face.

'Don't think I've ever had an ocean tug here before,' he said, 'I had to come down and have a look. I run the agency, and Than does the work,' he continued introducing me to a middle aged Malay man.

'Your tow is in Bohihan Island,' the Englishman continued, 'and I would like you to take Than, who will deal with the paperwork, and a customs officer as well.'

I looked surprised as the office had not given me any information.

'The ship is fully laden, but no crew on board. They were all brought back by the monthly small coastal ferry.'

'But what went wrong?' I asked. 'I am really surprised no one is on board.'

'There was an engine room fire, which they managed to put out, but nothing works, and the accommodation was partly damaged as well. Someone got himself killed, and the whole crew refused to sail.'

'What about the cargo?' I asked.

'Don't worry, the fire started just as they were about to leave. So the cargo was all secured ready to go, chain and wire lashings all tightened up. All you have to do is connect up and go,' the Englishman smiled.

'So she is a dead ship,' I said.

'Yes.'

'What about a towage certificate for insurance?' I queried.

'No one here for that and no one has said anything about it.'

'Okay, I will get the divers to secure the sea intakes and I will talk to the office on the radio.'

'You might as well spend the night here and leave in the morning. It is easier to see the reefs in daylight.' The Englishman laughed, 'so you can have dinner with us tonight. My wife would enjoy your company. We don't get many visitors here.'

It turned out to be a very jolly evening, the agent's wife obviously enjoying herself, just the three of us. She had made herself look pretty, hiding the washed-out look some women have when they live in the tropics for a long time, and she was wearing a colourful flowery frock. I was glad I had put on a clean white shirt and long white trousers. It was an excellent meal sitting at the table on the veranda overlooking the harbour well served by their servants dressed in spotless white uniforms. It was pleasantly cool after the heat of the day. I left earlier than I might usually have done because I had a pre dawn start in the morning, I needed to reach Bohihan island in daylight.

We left before daylight and I enjoyed doing my own pilotage out of the harbour. I found it very rewarding to have memorised the chart so I did not need it, although of course I made the officer of the watch put a position on every 10 minutes or so, just in case. The sun rose out of a smooth sea a fiery red which soon turned into a molten steel like orb which quickly heated the air making the day hot and enervating. I remained on the bridge for the whole passage because it was tricky navigation and at times we could see the coral bottom, the water was so clear. I would have to be careful with the tow to make sure that the towing wire did not drag along the bottom and snag the coral.

The densely wooded Bohihan Island rose out of the sea at some distance, its 780 foot high peak clearly visible in the late afternoon sunshine, its three satellites, two to the south east and one to the south west were sighted later, difficult to see at first. The four islands together make up the sheltered anchorage. The mangroves and coral reef surrounding the islands were seen as we slowly entered, the tow with its deck cargo of logs coming into view off the log pond by the manager's house on the south west tip of Bohihan island. The rusty steel stanchions on the side of the ship holding in the logs made her look ugly. It was only a few years earlier the place was raided by Filipino pirates, which was the reason for the lookout hut on stilts. I went straight alongside the Naru as the sun, hidden by the islands, set. The green jungle on all sides emphasised the rapidly approaching darkness giving the feeling of being encompassed by the islands. The light on the manager's house was the only sign of human habitation or presence.

Once safe alongside the Naru in the 69 position, the bow of the tug facing the stern of the ship, the crew started making the towing connection. The diver Elmo took myself and the two officials from Sandakan ashore in the rubber boat. We walked along the narrow path up to the house in the darkness, needing the torches we had brought with us.

He was the only European on the island, a big burly fellow with a very red face and a thick head of brown hair. He seemed very pleased to see us.

'I did not hear or notice you come in,' he said jocularly, 'finishing my afternoon nap, the heat you know,' he laughed 'you must join me for supper,' he continued looking at me.

He and I had a very enjoyable evening on the veranda overlooking the Messina, her deck lights lighting up the log pond. He was a very interesting man, much travelled to out of the way places and involved in a variety of different occupations.

Than and the Customs officer from Sandakan were honoured guests in the kampong where the loggers lived.

The next day, the divers sealed all the sea intakes and my crew finished connecting up the tow. The salvage crew tidied the accommodation, closing the cabin doors in the unburnt part and secured anything movable. The bridge was intact. The galley was gutted. The dry stores were partly burnt, but the fridges were a real problem full of rotting meat.

The Customs officer would not let us empty the contents into the harbour anchorage. I can't say I blamed him really but it created a very real problem for us.

The smell of rotting flesh, be it animal or human is quite awful. People who have not experienced it have no idea just how repulsive it is, the stink is nauseating, and it takes real courage to handle it slimy with that terrible smell and disintegrating, it is a truly horrible job.

That evening, the manager came on board for dinner his launch remaining alongside. The mess man Mickey covered my cabin table with my linen tablecloth, cut glass wineglasses, and we made a bit of a show, which surprised him, the Berry Bros wine even more so. I had Mickey dressed up in whites, and he looked very smart. We had quite a jolly dinner, and he told me about life in Borneo, which was interesting, if a bit lonely and a visit to Sandakan or Tawau was a real night out. He gave a fascinating account of the pirate raid when the RAF were called in and bombs were dropped.

'Oh by the way, I had a message from Tawau that some prisoners are still missing from that jail break the other day,' he threw out as he left the tug on his way ashore. I did not understand what a jail break in Tawau had to do with Bohihan island, and forgot about it. The Malay agent dealt with all the formalities and the Customs officer searched the dead ship after we were ready to sail, taking my bosun with him.

Javier was a big burly man, and very strong. The Customs man was happy, and I set sailing for daylight the next morning. We would be taking the agent and customs officer back to Sandakan with us, the coastal supply ship was not due for couple of weeks.

There would be no tug assistance for leaving, but I was not worried. I had to keep the Messina alongside to supply power to the windlass. Once the anchor was in the hawse pipe the mooring lines would be let go, the Messina moving off the tow and turning to head towards the entrance. The only really tricky bit was drifting once the anchor was off the bottom and the time it took to bring it home and secure. If we drifted too far I could always let go the tug's anchor although it was deep in the anchorage.

In the event starting at dawn there was no wind, and all went well. I towed on short stay through the narrow entrance and met a red rising sun presaging another hot day. The only problem was the rotting meat, if I entered Hong Kong with it still on board it was going to cause all sorts of problems with the authorities, and I needed to get rid of it, but I could not do so with the Sabah officials still on board.

The weather was fine and hot. The sun shone through a cloudless sky. I had no problem with the tow following well. I kept her on a shorter wire than usual in the calm sea, because in places it was quite shallow, as I had seen when coming in. I did not want the wire dragging along the coral bottom.

We dropped off the customs officer and Than outside Sandakan. The agent came out in his launch and took photographs, giving us a cheery wave. I set course north through the Sulu sea.

I discussed with Edgar, who was an experienced salvor, and the divers how we were going to get rid of the rotting flesh in the freezer. We decided that as the weather was so good I would bring the tug alongside the tow and the divers wearing their breathing apparatus would empty the freezer, and the crew dump it overboard.

It was a tricky manoeuvre the next day, but it was in deep water. The boatswain slacked off plenty of tow wire, I slowed right down and then stopped, just using the engine enough to keep ahead of the tow, while she slowed down slower then the tug. When the tow was almost stopped I turned the Messina with the tow wire slack and secured on the towing rail and headed back towards the Naru going alongside in the 69 position. The rubber big Yokohama fenders kept the two apart. I was quite pleased with myself as it was a tricky manoeuvre.

Once we opened the fridges the stench was truly terrible and I almost vomited, the blackened, decaying, rotting flesh was quite horrible and disgusting to handle. The divers wearing their breathing apparatus hauled the pieces including fish and carcasses out onto the deck and the crew threw it overboard. I agreed to a special bonus. It was one of the most unpleasant and loathsome jobs I've ever been involved in. Once emptied of the putrefying matter the fridge was hosed down, and using a portable pump the filthy water was pumped overboard. It took all day, the diving compressor on the Messina running to recharge the air bottles. The crew not involved had a great day fishing.

The tow continued through the Sulu Sea past Tabitha reef through the Mindoro Straits and out into the South China Sea. There was a tropical depression forming out in the Pacific, and I decided to make a final inspection of the tow in case rough weather prevented it later.

A day out from the Mindoro passage, the rubber boat was launched, and leaving Edgar in charge of the tug I went over to the tow in the rubber boat, Elmo the diver driving. The bosun and a sailor accompanied me. The Naru's freeboard was too high to get on board, but Javier had rigged the rope ladder with a line so he could lower it from the boat.

The logs were slippery from the morning dew, and I had to be careful. The bosun although big was fit and agile, as was the sailor, although much slighter, and they had no problem. It was already beginning to be hot the bright sun heating the air, the sea now had a silky shine, and then it happened. I slipped, coming back from inspecting the chain bridles. I stretched out my arm as I fell onto the log and put out my left shoulder. I was in agony, trying to sit up, clutching it. The bosun and sailor came over to me and looked down.

'My shoulder is dislocated,' I gasped, trying to put on a brave face in front of my crew. 'We have to put it in again or I can't return on board the Messina.'

She was hidden from me, sitting on the log, and seemed very far away in my present predicament. The fine morning seemed to mock me.

'Don't worry Cap,' said Javier with a grin. 'I am sure I can help you.'

The sailor looked askance because the bosun was a big man.

'I have done it before,' said Javier his mature brown face serious, 'but it will hurt.'

'Okay,' I said through gritted teeth, because it was extremely painful and I could not move my arm.

Javier lay me down on the log, telling the sailor, who looked really quite frightened, to hold my legs. He stood, one foot on my chest, picked up my arm and jerked. I screamed, but heard a click and knew the shoulder was back in place. The pain was intense, and then subsided. I gingerly tried to lift my arm, it was extremely sore, but I managed to move it. I looked up into the bright sky and gave thanks. Although I still could not see her the Messina did not seem so far away.

'Okay Cap,' Javier laughed, 'I am a good doctor.' The sailor gave a rather sickly grin, obviously glad it was over and it had turned out all right.

I said nothing but put my good arm out, so he could help me to my feet. I was looking forward and could now see my tug ahead and felt extremely thankful I would be able to get back on board. Javier was still looking at me when we heard a noise behind us.

I turned and saw two men standing on the logs, in front of the accommodation. I froze, shocked, still holding onto Javier's hand. Javier looked up, and I could see the alarm on his face. He let go my hand and said something in Tagaloc to the sailor.

The two men were not far from us, only a few yards and were holding what looked like crowbars. None of us had any weapons, except the knife Javier always carried in a sheath on his belt. The taller of the two men said something that I recognised as Tagaloc. Javier replied, and a conversation ensued.

He turned to me and said, 'they want you to land them. They are threatening to prevent us returning to the tug unless we agree.'

I massaged my shoulder, while I thought. 'Ask them where they got on the ship and why,' I told him.

Javier spoke, and after considerable interchange he started to inform me, when the diver's head from the zed boat appeared above the logs. He looked at the two parties, seemed to take in what was happening, and the head disappeared. A few seconds later, we could hear the roar of the engine and saw the rubber boat heading back to the Messina at speed, a white wash appearing on the now gleaming sea. The sun seemed hotter.

'Good man,' I said, 'gone for reinforcements.'

Javier nodded and said, 'they escaped from jail, along with a few others and managed to get on board in Tawau. They are Filipino cigarette smugglers, and they want to be landed in the Philippines.'

'Okay, keep talking; ask them how they got out of jail, where they hid on board, what happened when she was on fire, anything else you can think of. We will stall until Elmo returns.'

Javier continued talking to the two men in Tagaloc. The radio round my neck cackled into life. 'Sending six men armed with spears and knives and chains,' Edgar said crisply 'I am slowing down, and they will board using grapnels at the break of the forecastle.'

'Good man, well done Edgar,' I replied holding the radio in my right hand. 'There are only two of them, but they have crowbars.'

'No problem Cap we will fix them and rescue you.'

I could already see the Messina was closer as Edgar slowed down. It was the first time he had been in command of the tug, and he was rising to the occasion

155

magnificently. The Naru was slowing down, but carrying her way faster than the tug.

'Don't let the Messina get too close Edgar, keep well ahead of the Naru.'

'Okay Captain.'

Javier was still engaged in conversation with the two jailbirds. They seemed quite relaxed had lowered their crowbars and did not seem to realise what was happening, even though they were seafarers of a sort.

'Some of the prisoners managed to overpower the guards, and they took the opportunity to escape,' said Javier. 'Once onboard the Naru they hid in the forecastle so were not involved with the fire and managed to escape my search with the customs officer.'

'Keep them talking Javier, the Zed boat will be returning shortly with reinforcements. They don't seem to realise what is happening.'

Javier continued talking in Tagaloc. The sailor handed me his water bottle, and I gratefully took a sip. It was now really quite hot and I realised I was sweating profusely. There was no wind and the sun had turned the calm sea into liquid silver, harsh and bright.

The two stowaways heard the boat returning, I had seen it leaving the Messina leaving a white line on the water, and picked up their crowbars. They started to move in the direction of the ladder, they must have seen the divers head appear and disappear, perhaps they were not so stupid as I thought.

'Don't do anything,' I said, 'keep talking Javier. The sailor looked fearful and I whispered 'don't worry. Our people are coming over the bow.'

The rubber boat disappeared from view. The Naru was still moving through the water, but much slower. It was calm, with a very low long swell the shimmering water rising and falling gently as though the ocean was breathing, almost like a woman in repose.

A head appeared on the starboard side at the forward end of the logs wrapped in cloth, just the eyes visible. I could see the hands holding onto a rope, the thud of the grapnel hitting the log had been masked by the noise of the engine.

The two men could see what was happening and started to run forward but it was too late. My agile crew were on board, and moved swiftly over the logs towards me, shouting and screaming, waving an assortment of evil looking weapons. Javier shouted something in Tagaloc, and they dropped their crowbars. My piratical crew surrounded the two stowaways prodding them with knives attached to sticks and sharpened iron bars.

'Tell our people not to harm them,' I said loudly to Javier.

'They are upset because you were threatened and there has not been a fight to save you,' Javier laughed. I sat down on a log.

'Are you okay Cap?' asked Javier, concerned, his dark face wrinkled with worry.

'Thinking. Take me back to the Messina.' I ordered. 'I need to talk with Edgar.'

He helped me up, and I climbed over the logs, past the crew surrounding the stowaways, who were all gossiping away quite amicably, their lethal weapons laid down, and their faces uncovered. I was surprised to see Mickey the mess man, among them clutching a chain, and he smiled self-consciously as I caught his eye. The chattering stopped as I passed and said,

'I'm going back on board the tug to talk with the chief officer and decide what to do with these two,' I gestured at the two stowaways. They were both dressed in jeans and sweatshirts streaked with rust marks, which I suppose they must have stolen at some point. The taller one was obviously the leader, both had short cropped prison style hair and were lean and fit looking. They appeared quite relaxed, surrounded by my crew, who had got over their excitement.

'You stay here Javier and keep an eye on the stowaways. Take the tall one and a couple of sailors and search the accommodation where they have been living and make sure it is in order.'

'Okay Cap.'

Mickey stood up, swinging his chain and made as though he would accompany me back to the Messina. I climbed over the logs down to the ladder, Elmo passing me clambering into the boat to help me. Luckily it was only a short distance and there was almost no movement between the rubber boat and the ship both rising and falling on the low swell.

Edgar was on the tow deck, the towing wire secured on the tow rail, and helped me back on board the Messina assisted by Mickey. I was extremely grateful to be back.

'Go back and stand by the tow,' I told Elmo, and he sped away, the rubber boat planning across the still calm surface glimmering like ice in the now almost dazzling mid-morning sunlight. The slow throb of the tug's engine was loud in the stillness like a heartbeat making the tug a living being.

I slowly climbed onto the bridge and sank into the captain's chair massaging my shoulder, feeling weary yet stimulated by the outlandish events on the log carrier astern.

'What to do with them, Edgar?' I asked after I told him what the bosun had told me. Juanito was officer of the watch, his smooth face alert and trying not to show he was listening. 'There is no way we can turn around and head back for the Philippines. They say they are only cigarette smugglers. If we take them to Hong Kong there will be endless problems with immigration while they investigate and papers obtained. We would be delayed, and worse prevented from leaving if there was a salvage. Don't forget it is the typhoon season and you never know our luck.'

'Scarborough reef is on the way,' suggested Edgar.

'Scarborough reef,' I said, 'maroon them on the reef which is mainly underwater. That would almost amount to murder, Edgar,' I said rather coolly. Juanito looked shocked and Edgar snapped something in Tagaloc which made him move away.

He laughed, 'the fishing boats, Cap.'

'I must be going senile.' I laughed with him. Juanito looked surprised at our apparent mirth about such a serious matter, especially after being admonished by Edgar.

Mickey arrived and handed me a cold beer.

'What a good idea, that is what we will do.' I said enthusiastically. 'We will sail close to the entrance of the lagoon and run them in. That will be it; we will have washed our hands of them, because in Hong Kong stowaways are a nightmare without papers. Worse these people are self-confessed jailbirds, we remain silent and say nothing. Instruct the crew to keep their mouths shut. Has anything been entered in the logbooks?'

'Not yet, just the inspection of the tow,' replied Edgar and Juanito nodded.

'Good, we won't make any log entries about the stowaways.'

I felt a lot better, as Mickey handed me another cold beer, the outside of the glass moist.

'What were you doing with the rescue party?' I asked him.

He smiled sheepishly, his slight body curling up with embarrassment, and said quietly.

'I had to help rescue you Cap.'

'The chain?' I enquired.

'Very good weapon,' he said brightly, turned and walked away.

'I was astonished to see him, such a mild person,' I said to Edgar.

'Well, you see Cap I expect he has lived quite a tough life one way or another, and here he is a happy man, and his happiness was threatened.'

'What you mean Edgar?' I asked, surprised.

'He is happy on this tug; he has no ambition, being content with himself and content with his job. His happiness was threatened, if anything untoward occurred to you. He rose above himself to rescue you and so protect himself which is why I let him go. I was taken aback by his choice of weapon but supports what I say about his life.'

'I see,' I murmured, 'lucky man,' I mused, 'I mean having no ambition,' and went quiet for a moment.

'Okay Edgar to business,' I said briskly. 'Tell Javier to bring the stowaways to the tug, instructing him he is in charge of them until the reef. I don't think they will cause any trouble, but be alert. Secure the accommodation and remind him that there might be bad weather before Hong Kong if that tropical depression develops into a storm.'

'Okay Cap,' and he issued his instructions into the radio hanging around his neck.

Half an hour later, the rubber boat returned, fully laden with cheerful smiling faces, but in the calm sea it did not matter. The boat was hoisted on board, the second engine started and coupled in to the single shaft and full speed was resumed for Hong Kong via Scarborough Reef.

I was starting on my midday meal brought to me by Mickey, sitting on the bridge wing so I could watch the tow, when the two stowaways were brought to me. Jesus, the second officer, short and stocky and a bit slow, but very competent, and usually unflappable was taking his noon sight and seemed completely unconcerned by the jailbirds. He was more interested with his navigation, especially as I was not taking a sight, although Juanito was out with his sextant as well.

'They don't speak English,' Edgar informed me.

'I know. Tell them, no, better ask them if they agree to be put off on the reef, where they can join a fishing boat. After all, the reef belongs to the Philippines, or at least it is claimed by your government.'

'They don't want to go to Hong Kong. So yes, they will agree to be landed on the reef.' He spoke in Tagaloc to the two Filipinos, who nodded their heads.

'Okay, very good. I tell you what Edgar, just in case we have a problem later write up a note in Tagaloc with a translation in English and get them to sign it saying they wished to be landed on the reef. I will keep it in the safe.'

'Okay Cap.'

They left, and I enjoyed my curry lunch and a good afternoon sleep. My sore shoulder was a lot better.

The weather remained fine, almost no wind, although the low gentle swell increased a little the further that we proceeded from Luzon. The tropical depression in the Pacific had deepened and was now a named tropical storm and heading our way. Ricky, my conscientious radio officer, was obtaining regular weather reports from Hong Kong radio and Jesus kept a plot of her position.

The next day we came up to Scarborough Reef, the increased swell breaking gently on the coral and swirling over it. There was still no wind. Javier, brought the stowaway jail birds onto the bridge so that they could thank me.

'Ask them where they hid during the search in Bohihan Island.'

'In the fore peak tank,' he replied smiling, his rather severe face crinkling.

'Which accounts for the rust marks on their clothing,' I stated. 'Lucky the tank was ventilated enough or they could have died.'

Javier took them off the bridge and they sped away in the rubber boat, driven by Elmo. I watched through the big bridge wing binoculars. The rubber boat went right into the lagoon, past one of the fishing boats to a large boulder. The two stowaways scrambled onto it, just about big enough for the two of them, and the zed boat returned. While it was being hoisted on board I saw a small boat being paddled from the fishing boat to the boulder, and the waving stowaways. I waited until I saw them climb into the boat and at my last look the boulder was empty. My conscience was clear, I had not marooned them, but on the other hand I was not involved in their rescue, or escape. In my mind they had ceased to exist, the only evidence they had been on board my tug was in the safe.

I increased speed and wondered if we were going to beat what I was sure was a typhoon forming to Hong

Kong. A tow in a typhoon is something to be avoided at all costs.

I had a word with Fernando, the chief engineer, a large man and a bit of an old woman, but he always seemed to come up trumps. The speed increased sharply, and the Messina vibrated with the effort, as though she knew the coming danger and was thrusting forward with the power of her large single propeller. The swell increased slowly but noticeably and the tug pitched easily, the Naru also pitching, but following well. We made a good speed.

We reached Hong Kong in time to moor the Naru in the log pond. Discharge of the logs commenced using barges built with a single swinging derrick worked by powered winches.

The typhoon eventually passed quite close, and it blew hard and rained heavily, but that was all. It had been arranged to hand over the Naru to dockyard personnel after the bad weather had passed, who would complete the discharge while I shifted the Messina into the harbour for stores and bunkers.

A smart police launch arrived alongside shortly after anchoring and a smartly dressed inspector with a constable boarded.

'Good morning Captain,' said a very English voice.

'Good morning,' I replied, 'and how can I help you? I have never had a police inspector on my tug before.' I nodded to the Chinese constable, 'would you like tea or coffee or something colder?' I asked. It was mid-morning and hot, although the tall thin Englishman did not seem to feel it.

'No, thank you, Captain, this is an official visit,' he said quietly, but I felt the menace in his voice. My stomach lurched as I felt that first flicker of fear, but fear of what? I asked myself. The peak had a cloud cover over it; the harbour was its usual busy self, the passing typhoon forgotten, but I felt my world slowly turning over as though I was in a slow motion automobile crash. I waited for him to continue holding on to the bridge wing.

'I believe you have come up from Borneo, with a tow?' He asked, his rather thin lips moving slightly, his skin unusually white, his eyes very blue.

'Yes, the Naru, she is completing discharge in the log ponds.'

'I would like to see your logbooks, both the rough and fair copy,' he ordered, rather than asked, no please.

'Can you tell me what this is about Inspector?' I asked formally. 'My logbooks are not public documents.'

'Yes, yes,' he said testily, 'I have merely asked to look at them.'

I turned away from him to look at the water, made rough by the passing wallahs wallahs, ferries and

166

shipping, to think about it. I decided to go along with the Inspector, there was no point antagonising the police for nothing. There was nothing to hide in the log, we had done nothing wrong. Then it hit me. The stowaways.

Thank heavens we had omitted to log anything to do with them, and the entry when we dropped them off just said, 'reduced speed passing Scarborough Reef chief engineer request.'

I walked into the chart room and showed him the two documents.

'Perhaps my air-conditioned cabin, which has a table, would be of use to you,' I suggested.

'That is kind of you,' he said.

I settled the two policemen on the settee alongside the table and sat in my own chair which faced forward in front of a porthole. The Constable with his black hair studied the fair log while the Inspector, his blond hair neat and groomed, studied the rough. It was quite obvious they were looking for something.

After what seemed an eternity, but could not have been more than a quarter an hour, I noticed the tug had become very silent except for the noise of the generator, no voices, no sound of work on deck, as though the whole tug was in suspense, concerned, or perhaps frightened at the police on board.

Sometime later the Inspector closed the rough log with a snap.

'I see you stopped off at Scarborough Reef, on the way down and slowed down on the way back,' he stated crisply his unusually blue eyes boring into mine.

'Engine repairs, it is sheltered from the swell, if you're in the lee side of the reef,' I replied smartly.

'Did you have any passengers leaving Sabah?' He asked.

'Passengers?' I queried, 'certainly not.' I replied slightly riled.

'What I mean is, did you find anyone on the tow after you left?' His blue eyes held mine but they were not sparkling, they were not normal eyes, they had a kind of dead look despite their blueness and it was extremely intimidating. It was only years later in a very different situation I saw the same deadness, and it was the eyes of a skilled interrogator.

My mind was racing, and I had to make a conscious effort not to show any alarm on my face, not to sweat.

'No,' I replied firmly holding his eye which seemed to reach at my very soul.

Someone dropped something on the deck outside and I jumped, my nerves on edge. I stood up and looked down at him.

'A bit jumpy, aren't you,' he accused quite brusquely.

'Not at all,' I said, 'this is a salvage tug, and we are often in danger. Inspector, what is it that you are looking for?' I asked quite angrily. 'Keep calm,' I said to myself.

'Are you sure no one was on your tow?' He again asked looking me in the eye.

'No,' I lied firmly still looking down at him, the Constable watching, my heart was pounding and the palms of my hands sweating.

'There was some sort of jail break in Tawau and a murderer is missing.' He stood up, and I tried to conceal my shock.

'If there is anything you know which would help us, please let me know.' He handed me a card. 'Either, I, or one of my colleagues will be out tomorrow morning to have a chat with your crew. I noticed a couple of large sea shells when I walked through the accommodation. In the unlikely event you have to leave on a salvage, you must send a message to the police station.'

'He knew', I thought. 'Keep your nerve. Do nothing. Let them go and then think.'

The police boat sped away, and I called Edgar into my cabin.

'I am in trouble. The police seem to know about the stowaways, but I denied there were any. A murderer is missing from that jail in Tawau.'

He looked shocked.

'The crew will do whatever you say,' he said woodenly.

'I am sure we have done nothing wrong, however, lying to the police is a serious offence. That Inspector was no ordinary policeman. It was almost as though he could see into me.'

'Up to you Captain,' said Edgar unhelpfully.

'I don't think I have an option Edgar, even though this place is British. The police have their methods, and I would not like any of our crew to get hurt. Lawrence, the diver is a good sketch artist, get him to make a sketch of the two stowaways. I will take it ashore this afternoon together with their signed agreement. It is in the safe.'

'Okay Captain.' He looked and sounded relieved.

Mickey came in with a cup of tea.

'You've been spying,' I accused him.

He smiled, looking uncomfortable, and left. The crew would all know in a few minutes.

The Inspector was not in the police station at the address written on the card he had given me when I visited it that evening. I left the documents, with a short written note, in an envelope marked secret. I did not sleep well that night.

The police launch was alongside the next morning, at 0800, and the same two were ushered into my cabin.

'Never lie to the police,' he said harshly as he sat down.

I felt so small so humiliated, and it was all my own fault. Although I must admit I thought I was doing the right thing.

'Tea or coffee?' I asked quietly.

'Coffee for me and tea for Tan,' he said more brightly.

Mickey disappeared, and I thought of him swinging his chain on the Naru and shook my head.

'You are lucky,' he smiled, his thin lips parting slightly, but his eyes remained dead. 'Thank you for the sketch and signed agreement, wrong man. Case closed.'

* * *

The mariner finished his long story. We were all silent while we digested what he had told us.

'A quandary,' said the navy man. 'It was not very sensible to lie to the police. I wonder what I would have done in the same circumstances. I don't think leaving the stowaways on the reef was doing anything wrong. He was right about the problem they caused, especially in those years.'

'Perhaps not very sensible, but I don't think it was illegal,' said the lawyer. 'I would have risked bringing them to Hong Kong.'

'But you are not a salvor,' laughed the mariner.

'He seemed to forget the log book is a legal document recording all events occurring to the ship good or bad not a selective memory type thing. A judge would have something to say about omitting events.'

'I would have done the same,' said the banker firmly, 'no way I would want to bring stowaways and jail birds as well into Hong Kong.'

171

'Just as well he owned up,' said the navy man. 'I'm afraid the police might have bounced around his crew. That mess man was an interesting character, appearances can be deceptive.'

The banker snorted but remained silent.

'In the event, he was lucky,' said the lawyer. 'All is well that ends well.'

'Time for a drink,' suggested the navy man.

The beach was almost deserted except for a couple of lovers walking arm in arm along the shore, the children gone. It was slowly becoming dark, the sun had long disappeared the twilight fading into night. The yacht lay quietly.

10.

Trapus Reef

'It was rough and I was not feeling very well, not ill, just out of sorts with the world. I had delivered a barge, admittedly a big one and loaded too, to Hong Kong, but barge towing was not why I had joined a salvage company. We were running free southbound during the north-east monsoon and the only thing to look forward to was warmer weather. I was only using two engines to save fuel. It was reasonably comfortable with the wind and sea behind us, well it was on the port quarter. I intended to go close around Macclesfield bank, and do a bit of reef spotting further south, one never knew one's luck,' said the Mariner stroking his, what I thought was rather stupid, goatee beard, it made him look like some Spanish grandee. He continued.

'Richard gave me this account not long before he died, as though he was cleaning house before he went to meet his maker. He used to say he was one of the few people in the world to have been through the Pearly Gates and come back again alive to tell the tale.' He laughed, and said, 'but that is another story.'

We were sitting in the cockpit enjoying the spring sunshine, but it was cold with a fresh north east breeze blowing, which is what might have prompted the Mariner's memory. The yacht was anchored inside the creek, we had run in under headsail rounding up and anchoring, a nice neat manoeuvre which rather pleased us in our more mature years. Our lunch and a couple of bottles of wine were on the table.

'Well don't leave us in suspense,' grumbled the major, his white hair gleaming in the sunlight, 'we have all afternoon, even if we have to motor back.'

'As I said the north east monsoon was blowing strongly and they were running south a day or two out from Hong Kong,' continued the Mariner, 'and this is what Richard told me.'

* * *

Ricky, the radio officer, handed me a telex. We were the first commercial tug to have telex over radio but there was only one station, Berne radio which sometimes made it difficult. The message told me the company had signed an LOF, Lloyds Open Form, with the owners of the Wendy, not a usual name for a ship, aground on Trapus Reef, and gave the latitude and longitude.

Well my out of sorts feelings flew out of the wheelhouse door, this is what I had joined a salvage company for, not barge towing. I told the second mate, whose watch it was, to ring down to the engine room and start the other two engines. I sent the AB on watch to warn the chief officer and cook we were about to turn, and it would be rough, we had a salvage. Everyone was galvanised, I could feel it as the cough of a diesel starting indicated the second engineer was on the ball. I walked out onto the port bridge wing and looked aft to check for any traffic, the sea was empty.

I disconnected the autopilot, and turned the huge wheel, as tall as myself, to port. A second cough indicated the second engine had been started. The tug turned quickly, rolled, and I steadied her on the new north easterly course, reconnecting the autopilot.

She was now heading straight into the rough sea, and was already pitching into it, wisps of spray coming over the flared bow. I walked over to the engine control, on the starboard side at the forward end of the bridge, checked the newly started engines were connected to the two shafts, and slowly pushed the lever controlling both the engine speed and the propeller pitch. The Bashi, leapt forward under the thrust of her powerful engines and promptly shipped a solid sea right over the wheelhouse.

Woe up, take it easy, I thought, the casualty is aground, no point in smashing the tug up. Still, I wanted to reach her as fast as possible, every hour counted with a ship aground on an exposed reef. In this weather, unless they had something out to hold her, which I doubted, the rough weather would tend to push her further up the reef.

The quicker I could get there and connect the better.

The weather deteriorated on the passage north to a full north easterly gale, which did not bode well for the Wendy. The Bashi was shipping continuous heavy seas and I had to slow down, although we had put the steel storm shutters on the wheelhouse windows to prevent them being broken. The overcast sky during the day made the sea, covered in white horses, seem grey and uninviting and at night made the darkness seem much darker, no moon or stars, although the navigation lights of southbound ships seemed brighter, especially the red and green sidelights, pinpricks in the blackness, the white masthead like stars on the horizon.

Even, so, we made good time, I had remained on the bridge all night, and arrived at the north-west side of Trapus reef in the middle of the morning. The Wendy was not at the latitude and longitude I had been given but much further east, almost in the middle of the long northern edge of the reef, completely exposed to the elements.

My heart sank as I slowly steamed towards her, the echo sounder continually clicking as it made a paper recording of the depth of water under the tug's keel. It was quite shallow, and I altered course further off the reef, the Bashi rolling heavily and quite violently at times in the now beam seas. It emphasised her good stability, a bit stiff but all to the good in this kind of salvage.

Once opposite the stern of the Wendy my heart sank further into my boots. Edgar, my moon faced chief officer, Juanito, my good-looking second officer and Jesus, my dark third officer, were all with me on the bridge, while Pedro my overweight bosun was on the port bridge wing. They were all silent as we assessed the enormity of our task.

It was still grey and overcast, which emphasised the continuous white at the edge of the reef, the surf. The roar of the breakers, some of which seemed to hurl themselves at the reef, could clearly be heard. The waves were breaking on either side of the casualty, first hitting the stern in a smother of white spray, which covered the aft accommodation, and then sweeping along the sides of the ship before finally breaking near the bow. The loneliness and desolation of the place in the middle of the China Sea, many miles from any land, highlighted by the lack of any real marks or objects on the reef was made worse by the low cloud.

'No zed boat can survive that,' said Jesus, my best small boat driver, echoing my own thought.

I called up the casualty on the VHF and introduced myself to the master who answered. 'My name is Chris Thornton Captain,' he said.

'How long have you been here?'

'Four days,' he replied the VHF reception clear.

'Pity your owners did not inform us earlier, I could have been here two days ago.'

'I thought I could get her off on my own,' he said.

My officers shared the skepticism showing on my face.

'Okay, the details,' I ordered.

The Wendy had run aground during the night at her full speed of 14 knots. She was a log carrier of some 20,000 tons displacement carrying capacity, and had an aft draft of 15 feet when she grounded. The soundings round the hull indicated she was aground over most of her length, suggesting she had almost surfed onto the reef. There was only 18 or 19 feet around her stern and she had little or no ballast in her. Her engine was intact and everything was working.

'You are running light, empty, with no ballast?' I asked.

'Yes.'

It was not for me to criticise. I was here purely to assist and use my best endeavours to salve the Wendy, but it was no cure, no pay. In other words, if we were not successful the company received nothing and we got no salvage bonus. It was a good incentive to succeed.

'Okay, Captain Thornton, it is too rough to launch the zed boat, our rubber transport craft, and even if we were successful there is no lee, no shelter at your ship, so we could not get aboard. I would like you to back up the bitts you will use to make fast my tow wire, preferably wire lashings around the accommodation. The bollard pull of my tug is 120 tonnes and I can exceed that by various manoeuvres and we could easily pull out your bitts, if not backed up. While you are doing that I will run some soundings to see how close we can reach, my aft draft is more than yours.'

'Understood Captain, we will let you know when we're ready.'

'It was blowing a full gale now, the tops of the white horses were being blown off the waves filling the air with spume. The occasional bigger wave broke at the stern of the casualty with a sound like a clap of thunder, flinging spray right over her accommodation. The crew were going to get wet making the connection, I thought.

The Bashi slow steaming into the heavy sea was quite comfortable, but when I turned broadside on and proceeded parallel to the reef, she rolled a quick violent motion making standing up difficult. I had to hold on to something as did the others to keep on our feet.

I continued parallel to the reef about half a mile outside the casualty, the echo sounder making a paper tracing. At the eastern end, I turned and proceeded back a hundred yards or so closer to the Wendy, the water shoaling significantly until I finally decided I could not get any closer than about a quarter of a mile. Right off the casualty I closed in with the casualty bow on, as far as I dared, bow in so that if I did hit the bottom it was the bow, not my vulnerable propeller and rudder. It was nerve wracking work, but by mid-afternoon I had a clear picture of the area.

'Edgar, when we make the attempt I will go bow in as close as I dare. You will fire the Schermuly rocket, unless someone else is a better shot.,' I told my chief officer.

'I will do it,' said Edgar. 'I had plenty of shooting practice during the Vietnam war, although not with a line thrower,' his face was serious, his black eyes holding mine.

'We are dependent on the casualty crew to make the connection if you can get the line on board.'

'I think we should go in at a slight angle, so I can try and shoot the line over the accommodation, rather than fore and aft, where the waves might knock the line off the ship.'

'Good thinking, Edgar,' I said.

'Call up the casualty, Juanito and ask if he is ready,' I ordered.

The master answered confirming he was ready, but the crew were having a hard time of it on the after deck. Juanito informed him of our plan.

'Tell him he has got to be quick. I won't be able to hold the tug in position for long. There is a west going current running east to west along the reef.'

When all was ready, Edgar was at the bow. I crept in to the east of the casualty, my hand on the controls, the current setting me across her stern. The wheelhouse window was open. Juanito called out the soundings as we closed the reef. His voice suddenly raised an octave as he called out a sounding of 20 feet.

'Fire,' I called out to Edgar, who had the gun, which looked like a mini missile thrower, on his shoulder, the line in its box a neat coil, an AB steadying him. At that moment, the feeling a mariner never wants to experience occurred. The Bashi struck bottom. It was not hard, but I went full astern on the two engines. Edgar, who had fired the rocket making a whooshing sound, clearly heard over the sound of the surf on the reef, he almost fell and dropped the gun on the deck. The line appeared to be flying true and straight to the accommodation with the wind behind it.

The depth had increased enough, and I decided to make the turnaround, spinning the tug fast to starboard on her two engines. She took a tremendous roll to port, and then we were round heading out to sea. I rushed down the ladder onto the deck below, ran to the aft control position and switched over. I had her in position, the current setting her past the stern of the casualty. As I turned the men stationed along the port side of the tug let go of the rocket line so it was running over the stern of the tug, the end attached to the messenger rope. The Bashi was pitching quite heavily, but not rolling.

Edgar was the on the aft deck with the bosun. We were all trying to see if the rocket line reached the casualty, yes, it was over the accommodation as planned. Edgar had aimed well. It was just a matter for the crew of the Wendy to take hold of it, take it to a winch and haul in the messenger rope. Juanito was still calling the soundings from the bridge, using the loudhailer.

'Tell Wendy to get a move on.' I shouted at Juanito, so he could hear me over the noise of the engines, 'we are being swept past the casualty.'

I started altering course to stem the current, but now she started to roll heavily, the waves hitting the port bow. If I used power to overcome the current and put the bow into the sea she moved further away from the casualty. If I let her drift she fell off course, the waves pushed the bow round to starboard and the tug came broadside onto the sea. She then drifted towards the shallow water and reef rolling heavily. I could not understand what was taking the Wendy crew so long. We were now to the west of the casualty, and I was forced to use more power. I thought of using the anchor but rejected the idea because it complicated the manoeuvre.

Then I saw the rocket line go completely slack. They had lost it. I immediately put on more power and brought her up into the wind, signalling to Edgar to heave in the rocket line and recoil it in the box. I went back onto the bridge, and once I'd changed to bridge control handed over to Juanito. I called up the Wendy. The master answered.

'What went wrong, Chris?' I asked, my apparent friendliness hiding my seething anger.

'Don't know Captain, my men did not seem able to reach the line.'

'But it went over and was resting on the accommodation, it could not have been that difficult.'

'Well, they were not able to pick it up.'

'I am risking all for you Captain, I touched bottom and it would not take much more to lose the tug.'

'That's your risk Captain, not mine.'

I was filled with anger and rage and fought to keep myself under control.

'I will have one more attempt before it gets dark,' I said, 'make sure you have all available hands out. If the rocket line reaches your ship it is your responsibility to grab it and pull in the messenger. I cannot get any of my men on board, so you must do it.' I encouraged.

'My men are having a hard time of it.' He said.

'It will be a lot harder if we cannot connect and re-float you. Give your crew some incentive, offer them a bonus.'

There was silence.

'Just make sure you get hold of the line this time Captain.' I said firmly into the microphone.

I walked back and took over the controls from Juanito who returned to his station watching the echo sounder. It started to rain so I had to close the wheelhouse window and visibility closed in, but the wind was as strong as ever.

I repeated the same manoeuvre, this time without touching bottom. Edgar managed to fire the rocket true, which took the line over the accommodation. They must get it this time, I thought. But no, the same thing happened and I returned to the bridge wet through, angry and depressed.

A change of clothing and a hot mug of tea brought onto the bridge by my cheerful mess-man Mickey and I felt better. Juanito had been holding the Bashi in position astern of the casualty and I said, sitting in my captain's chair,

'Juanito steer west, keep half a mile off the reef. We will see if we can find a sheltered hole on the west side of the reef for the night.'

'Where are you going?' a voice came out of the VHF. I did not answer.

'You can't leave us,' the raised voice of the master said.

I still did not answer, and by now at almost full speed the heavily rolling tug was almost invisible from the Wendy in the reduced visibility for it was still raining. When I could no longer see the casualty the agitated voice said.

'I am reporting you to my owners.'

I picked up the microphone and said, 'tell them I am abandoning you for the night, due to your inability to pick up the rocket line.'

Once round the north-west corner of the reef and heading south it became quite calm both because the wind and sea were astern and shelter from the reef. We found a nice little bay in the reef and anchored for the night, enabling the cook to give us a good dinner. I ate as I normally did in my cabin.

The next day we were all were refreshed and even more importantly, the wind was down. I called a little meeting on the bridge after breakfast, the sun trying to break through the cloud.

'I noticed yesterday that there was a calm patch just ahead of the casualty.'

'Yes,' agreed Edgar.

'Enough water for the zed boat,' put in Juanito 'if I can reach there.'

'Yes well obviously not from outside the reef, but what about from inside. You can just see the casualty from here.' I suggested.

Juanito was an expert with reef work in small boats. He went out onto the bridge wing, and stared at the reef towards the casualty through the big binoculars on the stand. The sun occasionally broke through the south bound clouds which made it easy to identify coral heads above the water, but not below. Ideally, one needed the sun astern or much higher, to make out the danger under the water. Juanito walked back in.

'It's worth a go,' he pronounced. 'I will need Elmo in the bow so he can read the reef and Romeo the fitter to look after the engine.'

'Right Edgar, you are in command of the Bashi. The sea may be down, we will have to see. I am going with the zed boat. We will leave Jesus with you, but take Libre the other diver and two ABs. It will leave you enough to work the tug and make the connection. Ricky can watch the echo sounder for you and Jesus, who was also in Vietnam, can fire the rocket. We have two left, so make sure he fires straight.'

Edgar looked at me, a worried look on his usually smiling moon face, he seemed pale.

'I have handled her in fine weather,' he said, 'but not in weather like this.'

'Don't worry Edgar, I will be watching you like a hawk, make sure you have a walkie-talkie with you at all times. I will guide you, it will be just as though I'm standing next to you.' I said, the others on the bridge listening intently.

'I have every faith in you Edgar, and I know you can do it.'

Pedro, the portly but immensely strong bosun nodded his head, which Edgar saw.

'Divers to bring their diving gear, make sure we have a compass in case visibility comes in, check we have an anchor, sounding line, water, tools, you know the drill Juanito. Don't forget a spare propeller.'

'Okay Cap.'

'We leave in twenty minutes, you leave at the same time, Edgar.'

Mac walked up to Edgar, shook his hand and said 'you'll do fine Edgar, you know, you can rely on my engines,' he came over to me, shook my hand and said 'good luck Captain,' and departed the bridge, his thinning ginger hair the last I saw of him as he descended the bridge stairs.

It was a most odd feeling to be a passenger in the zed boat speeding across the coral reef, while my command was steaming outside, although I did have my walkie-talkie. However in my book, if I give what I think are tasks that a person can fulfil let them get on with it. I watched my tug carefully almost continuously. Elmo stood in the bow guiding Juanito with hand signals, and we reached the Wendy without incident.

The pilot ladder I had asked to be hung over the bow was not there. I called Edgar and told him to tell the captain to get his act together. The sea was definitely down, the waves were breaking earlier along the side of the ship, and there was a nice pool ahead of her, in which we anchored. The divers put on their gear and dived to have a look at the bottom of the ship as far as they could.

Eventually a head appeared over the forecastle coaming, followed by the pilot ladder. It was not easy climbing the ladder, hanging free from the flare, the overhang of the ship. The two ABs in the zed boat held onto it and stopped it twisting and I made it safely onto the deck of the Wendy. Although waves were hitting her stern she felt quite firm, too firm, I thought.

Once all my people were on deck, the boat at anchor, with a stern line to the ladder and one AB to help the divers, I said to Juanito,

'Sound the tanks and over the side round the ship. See what you can find out from the crew.'

'Okay.'

I made my way aft, past all the metal uprights at the side of the deck for securing the logs, to the accommodation. I was met by a Filipino crew man who showed me the way up to the bridge.

'My god, it's you,' I exclaimed aghast as I saw the captain, dressed in jeans and a sweatshirt. 'I did not recognise your name.'

'No but I recognised yours,' said Chris Thornton, unsmiling.

Once a bully, always a bully. I thought back to the cadetship I had the misfortune to sail in for one voyage.

'Well the past is the past,' I said, 'let's get on with the future and get you afloat.'

'I won't forget you ever,' he said forcefully, 'the trouble you got us into...' He stopped, taking a deep breath.

'Details Captain Thornton,' I said formally, 'can I see your soundings taken round the ship.'

He showed me and it was quite clear she was aground over most of her length as I surmised,

'Your ballast tanks are empty, you told me.'

'No, I filled them after grounding to prevent her going further up the reef. Yesterday the spray was coming right over the bridge.'

'Very good, when I have connected you can pump it out and that will certainly help the re-floating.'

I felt the ship shudder as a larger wave than usual hit the stern, and small droplets of water appeared on the bridge windows, salt caked though they were.

'The ballast pump has broken down, the chief is working on it now,' he said. My heart sank, if we could not pump out the ballast she would not re-float.

'When does the chief think he will have it repaired?' I asked quietly.

'Don't know, some spare parts may be missing.' He replied not apparently the least worried.

I went out onto the wing of the bridge to see how the Bashi was getting on. She was just coming up to the stern of the casualty and looked a fine sight, her white hull gleaming. What a big difference sunshine made, and the wind was down as well, although the waves were still breaking alongside the ship as far as amidships.

'Just hang off a while Edgar,' I ordered into my walkie-talkie, 'we have problems.'

'Okay,' replied his confident voice.

Juanito and the AB joined me on the bridge, looking at the tug, sleek and modern, her accommodation low above the white hull, a real ocean-going salvage tug. The orange letters on her side glistening in the sunlight.

'The crew don't like the captain,' reported Juanito, 'he bullies them and it's an unhappy ship. Yesterday he gave no instructions for picking up the rocket line. It seems he did not want them to grab it, although he did not actually say so. The chief officer is European and stays in his cabin. The chief engineer is okay and spends most of his time in the engine room. All the double bottom tanks and two ballast tanks are full, either water or fuel. Here is the sounding plan.' It confirmed the one Captain Thornton had shown me. 'The aft bollards are not backed up,' he added.

I looked at him. It meant that even if we had connected we would probably have pulled them out. It certainly seemed as if Thornton had an agenda which was different from mine. I would have to bypass him, and watch my back.

'We're going into the engine room Juanito,' I said.

He and the AB followed me. Once clear of the bridge I said, 'could you rally the crew and get the bitts backed up do you think?'

'Don't see why not, they don't like the captain, and if you stay on board, I think they would.'

'Okay, you do that and I will talk to the chief.'

I continued to the engine room.

'Hi chief, I am the Salvage Master from the tug,' I spoke loudly over the noise of the generators.

'Come into the control room.'

It was cool in the glass fronted control room overlooking the engine and less noisy.

'We can run down the ballast tanks without a pump.' He answered my question with a distinctive Geordie accent, 'but I can't de-ballast the water in four double bottoms.'

'If the ballast pump won't work, why can't you use the fuel transfer pump, they are all fuel tanks?' I asked.

He sucked his teeth. 'I would have to rearrange the pipework, which would bypass the oily water separator, and that's not allowed.'

'This is an emergency chief, if you don't de-ballast, we won't re-float.'

'I don't know why he ordered me to ballast them knowing I could not de-ballast. The pump is broken and a spare part is missing.'

I was beginning to wonder if there was more to this than met the eye.

'Your owners have signed a Lloyds form with my owners. I am in charge of the salvage, chief, and with your cooperation I can re-float you. I am asking you to de-ballast and we won't bother to tell the master. I am staying on board the ship until we have re-floated and will take full responsibility.'

He looked at me, weighing me up, I could almost see the debate going on in his mind, loyalty to his captain and ship, even though an unpleasant one, and siding with me, an outsider.

'Okay,' he put out his hand and I shook it.

'I will get the tug connected and once de-ballasted there is a good chance we can get you off the reef.'

I went out of the engine room and aft to the stern. No heavy water was coming on board, only the occasional spray, and I found Juanito, with the Filipino bosun. The crew seem to be working with a will.

'Edgar,' I called on the walkie-talkie, 'hopefully we are solving the problems but it will be a little while before we are ready. I am staying on the casualty.'

'Okay. We're quite comfortable here,' he laughed.

He sounds confident and in command, I thought and my spirits began to rise, helped by the bright sunshine and the prospect of possible success. The Bashi looked so powerful. The crew stopped work and were looking up. The captain was standing on the deck above glowering.

'Carry on Juanito,' I ordered sharply and loudly, and he spoke rapidly in Tagaloc. The crew turned and looked at me. I said, 'carry on. When you have finished we will connect the tug,' I smiled.

They took a last look at their captain and started work again. He disappeared into the accommodation. I felt I would have no problem with the crew making the connection, stiffened by Juanito, my divers and the AB from the zed boat.

Once the backup was completed, I called up Edgar and told him to make his approach. Juanito organised the Wendy and his own crew in strategic places to catch the rocket line.

The divers had dived as much and as far as they could and reported the bottom appeared damaged where they could see it. I was not surprised.

Edgar made a good approach, Jesus fired the rocket and Elmo the diver caught the line on the casualty. I had a willing crew, and I watched the Bashi like a hawk. The determined Filipinos on the aft deck led by Juanito made a quick connection. I did not have to make one suggestion to Edgar, although I wanted to micro manage and had to hold myself back. He was good.

'Well done Edgar,' I said into the walkie-talkie, 'and congratulate Jesus for his fine shot. Pay out 1500 feet and increase to three-quarter power,'

'Okay.' I could hear the spring in his voice as he replied. 'He is ready for promotion,' I thought.

'Elmo, go and get the zed boat on board. I am sure the bosun here will lend you some men, and you can use the derrick at number one hatch. Then come back aft and standby. You have a walkie-talkie.'

'Okay Cap,' he said and repeated my instructions.

'Juanito I need your moral support on the bridge. We will go via the engine room.'

'Ballast tanks almost empty, the forepeak's run down, and we're pumping the double bottoms, but it will take a few more hours yet,' said the chief engineer in the control room, his Geordie accent thicker in his enthusiasm.

'Right we are going to start towing. Is the main engine ready?' I asked.

'Yes, but I have a terrible feeling that the prop may have hit something after we grounded.' He shook his head and lowered it, his bald patch showing. 'He went astern on the engine, and I'm almost sure, but the waves and the noise and the shuddering,' his voice petered out.

'Right, we will only use the main engine as a last resort,' I said.

On the bridge Captain Thornton was sitting in his captain's chair, the chief officer, who looked as though he was on something, standing nearby. I decided to ignore them.

'Edgar, increase to full power and steer straight astern,' I said into my walkie talkie.

'Okay Cap.'

I watched as the tow wire lifted momentarily out of the water and then settled back. I looked forward and saw the zed boat was already on deck. Ahead of the ship was a slight oil sheen, the chief engineer pumping out the ballast from the double bottoms. Thornton had ordered the empty fuel tanks to be ballasted.

'You using the main engine?' asked Thornton.

'No,' I replied.

I saw no reason to engage in conversation. He had not tried to interfere with me yet. He must have known the crew were on my side, and this was the first I'd seen of

195

his chief officer. The weather was quite good, sunny and blowing about force five to six. The sea was well down, which in some ways was a pity. A big wave might just have been enough, and given her enough buoyancy to re-float with the big tug towing at full power. The twin propellers were creating a healthy white disturbance at her stern.

'Everything okay Elmo,' who was back on the aft deck.

'Okay Cap no problems.'

'Don't forget to keep greasing the fairlead for the tow wire.'

'Okay Captain.' He managed to inject into those two words that he knew what he was doing, and Juanito who had heard the exchange smiled.

'What about some sandwiches?' I asked Captain Thornton, who grunted. At that moment, the chartroom door to the accommodation opened and a smiling Filipino came in, bringing a tray, with a huge pile of sandwiches and pots of tea and coffee.

'Who ordered that?' snapped Thornton in a rage, his face red.

The messman just smiled, put the tray on the chart table and departed.

'Tuck in Juanito,' I suggested.

I noticed the ships log was missing from its usual position on the chart table.

'We had better get some bearings to tell us when she starts to move Juanito. There are a few coral heads we can use. I estimate high tide to be in a couple of hours.'

He went out onto the bridge wing and noted the bearings taken with the gyrocompass in his notebook.

'Better have a helmsmen standing by,' I suggested to Thornton who grunted. I was not too worried. Juanito could take the wheel, or I could call up one of my ABs.'

An hour or so later, there was a click, the sound of the gyrocompass moving. It was only one click, but I felt galvanised, and I saw Juanito had heard it too. He checked his bearings but shook his head.

'Elmo send an AB to the bridge,' Juanito ordered into his walkie-talkie. Thornton had not taken up my suggestion. I smiled when I saw which sailor appeared, the biggest and toughest of the two.

'Stand by the wheel Javier, and let us know any change of heading. The rudder is amidships,' and I pointed to the rudder indicator ahead of him on the bulkhead.

The sheen of oil was flowing forward of the Wendy, so I presumed the chief was still pumping out the ballast. There was another quite audible click from the gyro and Javier called out,

'One degree to starboard, course 201.'

Even Thornton looked interested and interrupted his conversation with the dazed looking chief officer. I went out onto the port bridge wing, blinking in the bright sunlight.

'Edgar tow out on the port quarter. We might have the beginnings of movement. One hour to high water.'

'Okay Cap.'

I saw the Bashi turn to starboard and head out onto the port quarter of the Wendy. There was plenty of water out there. I watched the tug heel over to starboard and the tow wire came out of the water as the tug moved sideways through it, adding the weight of the tug to the towing power. The tug straightened up, the tow wire momentarily almost came out of the water and then settled back.

'205' called out Javier, '206, 207,' and then silence.

Juanito on the bridge wing watching his bearings shook his head.

'Why not use the main engine?' asked Thornton gruffly, as I walked back into the wheelhouse.

'No,' I replied strongly.' I don't want to further damage the propeller.'

'Who says it is damaged?' he demanded brusquely

I remained silent and walked back out on to the bridge wing with a mug of now almost cold tea. Thornton was very uneasy and I wondered why.

'Edgar,' I said into the walkie-talkie, 'swing slowly round to the starboard quarter and then back again, as we did with the Dortmund. I will watch you, don't forget that the current is setting you to the west so turn early.'

'Okay Cap,' was the rather laconic reply, indicating without saying so he had not forgotten about the current.

I watched him turn the tug to port and swing all the way round to the starboard quarter. It was quite clear, he knew what he was doing and confident enough to do it. I need not worry about him, Captain Thornton was the problem.

'206, 205, 203, 201, 199,' sang out Javier, and then she stopped.

Suddenly I heard more clicking noises, but they were not from the gyro, followed by the hiss of compressed air, and the main engine started. I sprinted into the wheelhouse and over to the electric engine room telegraph, which was on the starboard side and pushed the lever back to stop. It was too late. The engine had started, and there was a tremendous shudder as the engine stopped. The engine room telephone rang and was answered by the chief officer.

'Engine room says possible shaft damage. The propeller hit something.'

'You fool,' I shouted at Thornton. He smiled and said nothing.

'Do not do anything unless I tell you. I am the Salvage Master in charge, and this will be reported to your owners.'

The Bashi was swinging back and Javier was calling out the heading. When the tug reached the port quarter she turned, the heading reaching 215. Broken coral was running forward, clouding the clear water under the oil sheen white.

The Wendy continued to swing. The heading increased at each turn the tug made, until just after high water with a shudder she slid off the reef in a cloud of coral, and suddenly came alive.

It was an uncomfortable tow stern first into the shelter at the western side of the reef, where the Bashi was disconnected and then reconnected to the bow of the Wendy. The divers reported considerable bottom damage but no apparent holes only deep dents. I foolishly went back to the Bashi and sent Edgar to take charge of the casualty.

On the tow to Hong Kong a fire started in the galley and the whole accommodation went up
in flames. It was eventually put out by the crew led by Edgar, but too late to save much. Thornton was found in the forecastle, confirming that bullies are often cowards.

On arrival in Hong Kong, I confronted Thornton.

'You deliberately tried to prevent the salvage,' I accused him 'and the fire is most suspicious. What should have been a successful salvage has turned into a disaster with a burnt-out accommodation and damaged engine and propeller.'

'Pay you back to what you did on the cadetship,' he said vindictively.

'You are deranged,' I said angrily and left the Wendy. I never saw Thornton again.

Once everything was settled, the Wendy alongside at the dockyard, and the Bashi at anchor on salvage standby I went ashore in the junk attached to the tug. The mama san wished me well as I stepped ashore and made my way to the Marine Department. The head of the department had also had been on the cadetship, a first tripper like me.

I took him out to an expensive lunch in the Mandarin Hotel and told him everything suggesting that Thornton had in fact, cast his ship away and certainly ruined my salvage. The ship was almost certain to be declared a total loss thus of little salvage value, scrap only.

'Well, well. Thank you for that Richard, excellent lunch. The info will help in my enquiry into the grounding. The owners are a dodgy lot, and it would suggest they might have put him up to it. We will see. Rest assured, Captain Thornton will never sail as master again. I have not forgotten the cadetship my friend.'

* * *

'And that was that,' finished the Mariner.

'So Richard broke Thornton's rice bowl,' suggested the naval man.

'No. Thornton lost his ticket, but became a surveyor instead,' the Mariner laughed.

'The devil looks after his own, but it was not a first-rate outfit, very down market.'

'So Richard did not get his revenge after all,' said the naval man.

'Deliberately casting away a ship is a difficult thing to prove,' put in the lawyer.

'Yes,' said the mariner, 'but the owners got their total loss, not their first or last. You wonder why underwriters insure them with their record. Thornton was not a happy man, his wife left him and he finally died on a ship he was surveying in what might be termed as mysterious circumstances,' said the Mariner.

'It's cold, let's motor home,' grumbled the major.

28766584R00118

Printed in Great Britain
by Amazon